Scars on my Soul

Scars on my Soul

Ritu Chowdhary

PARTRIDGE

To order additional copies of this book, contact
Partridge India
000 800 10062 62
orders.india@partridgepublishing.com

www.partridgepublishing.com/india

In loving memory of my mother…

After every storm the sun will smile; for every problem there is a solution, and the soul's indefeasible duty is to be of good cheer.

William R Alger

Acknowledgement

I would like to thank my family, and friends for their relentless support and encouragement.

I'm highly indebted to Puneet and Neerja for reviewing the book, and extending their support in editing it.

It won't be fair on my my part if I put down the pen without giving special thanks to my daughter, Anya. On several instances, she has gone beyond her age of five to understand the blocks I was facing. Her enthusiastic suggestions are always great motivators.

Finally, my thanks to everyone, who has been with me through the course of this book.

Chapter 1

10th Aug 2009, Monday: 'Adie, you have a video conference at nine with Brian.'

'I know; anyways, thanks for reminding.'

'Hey, Nikki! Are you not staying back?' I call out, as she scurries towards the door.

'Sorry Adie. My son has called me up five times. I need to be with him. I'm already late,' she says, standing in the doorway

'It's okay. You take care,' I remark with indifference.

My friends call me Adie, I work as a Director for an American bank; Nikita– Nikki, is my personal assistant; a perfectionist, and a thoroughly professional lady.

Aadir Chopra is the name imprinted on my credentials. The mirror reflects me as a young and a charming man; women swoon over my styles. I'm surrounded by fairer sex more than often, and the fact is, I too like to see them around, though, I always maintain a distance. I'm thirty-two, and separated; but yet not in the list of eligible bachelors. I'm still legally wedded.

The day ahead is hectic. I'm working on a presentation for VC today. Brian is a tough guy. He wants to dig into the nitty-gritty of each proposal, so I'm working on the minutest details. He's obsessed with creating value, and on my end, I abhor exhortation and criticism. Anyways, why should I accept crap from anyone when God has made me a perfect man with hardly any scope for refinement!

Nikki's gone for almost half an hour now. I dial *101* on the intercom– Nikki's extension number; my fingers scamper on the phone keys as if this is the best tune I can play on my piano. There's a beep, but no response. I'm unable to control myself to call out her name– 'Nikki, Nikki,' but soon I realize that she isn't around. I feel frustrated without her.

I'm feeling peckish; I wish if I can have something to munch. Nikki takes care of my breakfast and lunch in the office, and I usually dine out if there aren't any plans to skip the dinner.

No! Taking care of my food, isn't part of Nikki's official duties, but she's overly concerned about my personal welfare, so she does it willingly.

Oh! My stomach feels clenched; my eyes are dull and contracted; there's sprinkle of sweat on my forehead. I can't focus on the presentation any longer. I move out to the smoking zone. I have become extensively dependent on nicotine and Nikki. I know Nikki from a distance, and our relationship has been a stereotype of a boss and a subordinate, except her concern about my eating. I have a vague idea about Nikki's personal life that, she has a broken marriage, and proceedings for her divorce are on. She has a six-year-old son, and she's too protective of him.

A puff rejuvenates me. I move back to my room to work on the presentation. The empty seats; switched off lights and a lull in the office reminds me of my life. I feel lonely and depressed; the way I have never felt in the past. I want to rush out of the plush office. But, where? Back to my royal house with immaculate interiors! Apart from the exclusive tastes of the owner of the house, the place symbolizes loneliness.

Perhaps, I'm mentally exhausted. As soon as I reach my room, I switch on the music and lie down in my stylish chair, with head stretched backward; and before I even realize, I drift into slumber.

* * * * *

"'I'm flying with Singapore Airlines on the twenty-eighth, come to pick me up at eleven o'clock and no car, please. I'm dying to ride on my beautiful, Hyosung. It's been a while, I have started feeling like an oldie– decked up in formal suits and traveling by MRT. I want to feel young for these three days.'

'Don't worry! You are going to be on cloud nine, Akanksha too is joining us for the reunion. She has informed the organizer that she's coming along. I feel you still have a chance.'

'I'm sure we are going to have a gala time.

'Okay, bye for now. See you on the twenty-eighth.'

I was excited about the reunion of my batch in Kolkata. I wished if I could give a bump on Charlie's head at that very moment, this was the way we greeted each other. Charlie was my ace buddy in college. So much so that I decided to give up chasing Akanksha, college hottie when I realized that Charlie too had a crush on her. Unfortunately, after chasing her for six months, he was dumped for being a Chatterji– Bengali. She was a Punjabi, looking for a boy from her own clan as she thought life gets simpler with a person from a similar culture. By the time this episode unraveled, I had become more interested in campus placements rather than pursuing Akanksha, or maybe I was never too keen on her.

Charlie's father was a dominating personality, and Charlie would have never mustered the guts to go against his wish of, being at home in Kolkata with the family. Akanksha was fortunate, or a visionary, not to accept Charlie's proposal.

Besides the fear of his father, Charlie was an intrepid guy; whether it was protesting in school for a cause or confronting girls, he used to lead. Though, he belonged to an Orthodox family, he always professed tolerance and respect towards every religion. I couldn't understand what happened to him in front of his father, he was dumbstruck.

28th Nov 2007 11:00 p.m.: Charlie was at the *Netaji Subash Chandra International Airport*. I was excited to meet Charlie after two years; but more than that, I wanted him to quickly hand over *Spicy Chicken Wings* from my favorite restaurant–*Flame and Grill*, on Park Road. I was a complete no-no to the vegetarian food; and an ardent lover of non-veg. Chicken in any form and a bottle of Cabernet Franc or any other wine was sufficient or essential, for my survival.

There came out me; tall, broad, fair complexioned, green eyed; a young man with ravishing looks and casually dressed in a white tee and blue jeans. Charlie rushed towards me, and for a moment, we prepared for the *bump on the head* greet. This time, it became a bit forceful from me, and Charlie had a little bigger hump on the head. Don't be worried! It happened every time; it was an intimation to our friends that we have met after a while. At least now, Charlie would be saved from the stress of answering to everyone that when I would be around. His face would show it all.

After a round of hugs, Charlie rushed me to his bike where Chicken Wings were waiting for me in a saddle bag.

'What an aroma! There couldn't have been a better welcome than this. Where's the wine?'

'Are you crazy? You are going to meet Ma and Baba after a few minutes, how can you drink just before meeting them.'

'Hey Charlie, this has been always a bone of contention between us. I don't think drinking or eating, whatever you desire, lessens the respect for anyone. Respect is in your heart and mind. Moreover, I never drink in excess so as to lose control over myself.

'Leave it! I never understand why people can't do away with hypocrisy, and simply be what they are; especially, you Charlie. Bro, change yourself before it gets too late, no girl is going to accept you with these idiosyncrasies.'

'My dear Adie, let's not start it again. You are here for three days; let's juice the lemon to its fullest.

'I'm sure, no one else but life will teach you that sometimes it's not bad to be hypocrite if it pleases someone.'

'Crap, crap...

'Let me enjoy the chicken and I'm not interested in your nonsense. I'll definitely visit Ma and Baba but not today, it's too late; tomorrow will be okay. And, please ensure they don't insist on any grassy lunch. I can't take vegetarian food, and by no means, I'm interested in visiting a gastroenterologist if they succeed in walking me into a trap.'

'Good, you aren't going. If you meet them now, they can even smell your chicken. You know, how averse they are to non-veg and alcohol.'

'Fantastic! I'm your friend and not family. I don't know what I would have done in that insane environment.'

'Here you are, at the *Hyatt Regency*. The other guys will arrive in from Thursday. Still, we have a day at our disposal. Let's plan the itinerary, and also, discuss Akanksha.'

'Not now, let's do it tomorrow. I also need to call Muma before its too late.

'Wake me up in the morning, whenever you come.'

'Spoilt brat; at least, you have started caring about Muma.'

I was carrying two big suitcases for five days. I out passed any girl, when it came to taking clothes and shoes while traveling. My world would stop if I didn't change my attire, at least, three times before giving it a go ahead, and then I was too finicky about footwear as well. I entailed a suitcase for shoes and grooming products. I wanted nothing less than a perfect look.

I entered the lobby and headed towards the reception. There was hardly any eye which didn't move to have a glimpse of mine.

'Good evening, Sir,' a gorgeous girl on the reception greeted me with a charming smile.

'Hey, Aadir Chopra.'

She keyed my name in the computer, 'Aadir Chopra, you are here for alumni meet.'

'Yep.'

'You are booked with us for three days in Diplomatic suite.'

'Right ma'am,' I said in a respectful tone. I was a thorough gentleman, dignified in my behavior with the womenfolk, and I think it made me all the more appealing.

'Here's the key– Room No. xxx. Sir, have a nice and comfortable stay.'

'Thanks, Good Night.'

I entered the big luxurious room stretching 120 sq m in the area. I was stunned to see outside of the floor to ceiling windows, the spectacular view of Kolkata. Things were different as a student, three years ago *Hyatt Regency* in Salt Lake City was a distant dream, and it seemed in a wink of an eye, I had accomplished so much. I never expected too much from life. I was a happy lot, but as long as no one intruded in my freedom.

I was delighted to be there. Immediately, I ordered red wine, and butter chicken with bread. I partially unpacked the bags, it was like the beginning of the chaos. I attacked the Jacuzzi in my room, and once I had loosened up, I called up Muma, and as usual, my Muma was thrilled to listen to my voice. Hardly had we talked, Muma broached the subject of my marriage.

'Relationships change over time. A few girls, you don't like when you are studying with them, but they appeal to you once you are out of the college. I have seen so many girls and boys, who never bothered to talk to each other when they were studying together, and they propose after putting away. Though, I don't find it's a good fit for you, but I'll be happy if you can find a girl even in your own group.'

'Muma, I'm impressed. Your thoughts are enchanting.

'BTW, why did you say it won't be a good fit?' I said with lines on my forehead.

'Adie, I know you are a freedom freak and headstrong too. It's difficult for girls of your profile to tolerate this deadly combination. They too are impatient, like you,' I could imagine Muma smirking.

'Muma you are rating your son too low. If, Adie is the guy, no girl would like to be anything else but Adie's wife.'

'Come out of your fantasy world, my son. I'm living in this institution for the last thirty-two years and I know it better than you,' Muma had an authority of experience in her voice.

'So, what breed of girl do you think can be my wife?'

'Intelligent, patient, flexible, loving and above all, who respects the institution of marriage.'

'Muma, at times you are too jocular. I have landed a few minutes back, and I am a bit tired too; but asking me to marry was the first item on your priority list, and at the same time you are suggesting me to marry an alien, who'll be impossible to locate.

'I think, you are tired too. When I meet you on Saturday, we can discuss it in details.'

'But don't miss out any good opportunity in between sonny,' Muma quipped.

'Have faith in me.

'How are Rachel and papa? Is Rachel coming back this weekend?'

'Papa is eager to meet you, and Rachel is irked as she won't be able to make it.'

'I'll miss her.

'Good night Muma, and dream about me, not my marriage,' I hung up the phone to answer the bell at the door.

'Please come in.'

'Your dinner, Sir,' Waiter said, as he entered the door.

'Thank You. Set it on the table,' I spoke from the Jacuzzi.

Butter chicken smelt too yummy. The entire room was freshened up with its aroma. I came out from the bathroom, and without a second's delay attacked the sumptuous food.

After having the dinner, I jumped into my king size bed, and Muma's words echoed in my ears. It struck me that truly,

I had never tried visualizing a girl with whom I would like to spend my entire life. I was very popular among females. I had several gorgeous, successful, intelligent girls in my circle, but no one had really touched my heart. I pondered; I would prefer a girl with stunning looks, smart, fun loving, and caring like my mother. My mind wandered towards Akanksha, and I started exploring my heart. While I was thinking, sleep crept into my eyes.

29th Nov 2007: Phone buzzed, but I was undisturbed. Charlie was getting furious, waiting at the reception. It was audacious on his part to have come at 8:00 a.m., especially, on a holiday; he knew HYPNOS is residing in me. Charlie was also a hard nut to crack, so he waited there; though, impatiently, for two hours till I picked up the phone.

'You asshole! Open the door. It's been two hours I'm standing here.'

'Don't they have cafes here; you should have had some breakfast. Without fail, we are visiting some doctor today to get your insomnia treated,' I said in a weak voice.

'Shut up! And open the door.'

'Okay! Drag yourself in.'

'Shit man! Nothing has changed. You are still a leech. Look at the mess you have created in the room,' Charlie said, as he entered in.

'Are you planning to clean it up? If not, just chill!'

'Why should I? Akanksha is there to do the honors.'

'Gauche! Have you told her about me?'

'You are a bastard! Akanksha is arriving today night, but I can see the level of androgens rising in you.

'I came early; since Ma, Baba and Ananya are eagerly waiting to meet you. Now, they have left for Presha's college. Anyways, we are going to her dance program now so you can meet everyone there.'

'Presha?'

'My cousin– younger uncle's daughter.'

'Where did this uncle come from?'

'I'm talking about Kailash uncle; he was on an assignment with FAO in Budapest. Last year he retired, and now he's staying in our ancestral house with us. Presha is his only daughter; she did her high school in Budapest, and after that, uncle wanted her to join some girl's college in Kolkata for graduation.

'Hurry up! Get ready. We need to be there at *Gokhale Memorial Girl's College* in an hour; otherwise, Presha is never going to talk to me if I reach late. She's too attached to me; she won't perform unless she finds me in the auditorium.'

'This is quite emotional.'

'I'll try to get my act together in half an hour,' I scoffed.

'It sounds too ambitious, but still I'll like to believe it. I'm sitting in the cafeteria. Let's see, how deadline oriented, you have got.

'See you,' Charlie banged the door and darted out, to give sufficient time to me.

I was utterly confused. I stumbled on what to wear; as that day, I didn't have the luxury of dress rehearsal. I chose to wear a stone washed denim jeans and a black T-shirt. I splashed on a little *Blue De Chanel*, and there I was– a young, sanguine and charming man, capable of taking away any woman's breath.

I joined Charlie in the cafeteria, had a frugal breakfast; we started for *Gokhale College* on Charlie's bike, where Presha was to perform in half an hour. I was bewildered by my act– I was going to a girl's college to watch a dance performance. Absolutely absurd! But I couldn't have said *no* to Charlie.

Chapter 2

As soon as the bike entered the campus, it seemed as if a swiveling movement was programmed in every head. Girls vied to get a glimpse of the hunk entering the college. All the more, since my looks were quite distinct in the crowd; unusual from classical Indian looks.

There we were, in the college auditorium. Ananya had a frisson of excitement, as she caught the whiff of my perfume and knew I was around.

'Dada (bro)!' she screamed and got up from her chair to rush towards me.

'How are you, Lil?' I gave her a tight hug.

'You have grown into a typical Indian beauty. Gorgeous! Where's Baba?' I moved towards Ma and Baba.

Ma and Baba were also exhilarated to see me as if I was their second son. I touched their feet and they embraced me.

'Baba, only if you allow me, should I look for a suitable match for Ananya tomorrow? There'll be many well settled eligible bachelors in the party.'

'No, no. I only want a Bengali Brahmin for her.'

'But, Baba even I'm a Punjabi. Don't you like me?'

'You are our star, our son; but son-in-law and daughter-in-law should be of the same religion and caste. Otherwise, life gets complicated due to different cultural values.'

'Baba I know you are the best judge,' I knew it was no use arguing with Baba as he was too stiff and traditional in his thoughts.

I turned around towards Charlie, 'You swine, should I tell Baba about you and Aki?'

'Oh! Now she's your Aki,' Charlie remarked, ducking the peril he felt even at the thought of what I said.

'Is there something important, which I need to know,' Ananya poked, as she held my hand dragging me to sit with her.

'Dada, anyways, you are here for a short time, and still you aren't focused on me.'

'Lil, I'm all yours. Tell me, how can I please you?'

'You were asking Baba something regarding me. You have my go ahead. If you want, I can accompany you.'

'Shut up! Your brother is terrified by Baba, and you are entirely unruffled.' The guts of the girl had always amazed me.

'That's why you are my beau idéal of life and not Charlie. You should have a spine to speak for yourself,' Ananya spoke with sparks of revolution in her eyes.

'Shsh…show is about to start. We can discuss it later.'

It started with a boring welcome speech, hardly anyone was interested in. *Kathak* performance by Presha Chatterji raised the curtains for the show. As soon as Presha's name was announced, there was exuberance in the environment. Whoops of delight by girls and a few boys, seemingly from some neighborhood college, made the auditorium peppy.

I was bowled over to see such a freaky response from the crowd. 'Your sis seems to be an aristocratic personality of the college,' I said to Ananya, who too was going berserk.

'She's a heartthrob. Oh! There she is.'

A tall, slim, beautifully proportioned girl with long raven hair tied in a plait swaying below her waist, appeared on stage to perform solo Kathak dance. Her dark, big and bold eyes, with crisp movements, were a pleasure to watch. She wore a cream colored saree, accentuating her tan color skin peeping through her dress.

Onlookers got euphoric. I was indifferent; classical dances never caught my attention, and above all, my motto of going there was just to meet Charlie's family.

'Dada, I feel Presha is being distracted by you,' Ananya muttered looking at me.

I was stumped by Ananya's remark, but I held my tongue tight and preferred to glance at Presha before commenting. Presha seemed charmed by me and was surreptitiously looking at me. Her body language suggested she was eager to meet me.

'She's just inquisitive,' I said, keeping my decibels low.

'I can see it,' an impish smile crossed Ananya's face.

I soon got busy with my iPhone, avoiding on purpose to look at Presha.

The crowd gave a standing ovation to Presha's dance performance. I finally raised my head up when I felt she was out of sight.

I bid adieu to Charlie's family and moved out of the auditorium with him, Ananya accompanied to walk us to the parking. While we were moving towards the bike, Charlie was busy bird watching and Ananya chatted with me.

'Charlie! Charlie!' It was Presha rushing towards us.

Hey, Lil, you were fabulous,' Charlie hugged Presha while she was stuck with me.

'Dada, is he Adie?,' Presha said coming straight to the point.

'Oh, sorry, I didn't introduce you guys,' Charlie said, getting a little embarrassed on Presha's over-eagerness.

'Presha barely gave you any time, she seems to be running too fast,' Ananya said with a wry smile.

'Stay quiet,' Presha said rebuffing Ananya.

'Hey, Adie! I'm Presha,'

Charlie couldn't hide dismay on his face, but then, I winked at him to keep his cool.

'Hello Presha, you were spectacular!' I said, holding out my hand towards her.

'You are quite a pseudo. You just looked at me,' Presha commented enthusiastically.

It was overstretching for Charlie; he admonished Presha to hold her tongue. Charlie was perplexed with the ebullient behavior of Presha. He was afraid I might find her flirtatious, and he knew, I kept a low opinion about the coquettish girls. Charlie was a typical older brother and wouldn't have tolerated anyone considering her sisters sleazy.

'Dada, let's go out for lunch,' Ananya said, helping her cousin, who was undoubtedly falling for me.

'No, Ananya, we already have some plans for the day, and moreover, we're on a bike; you can't come with us,' Charlie out rightly dismissed the idea.

I softened, looking at Ananya's dismay. I didn't realize, but I too had started paying attention to Presha, and a frown on her face prompted me to say, 'Charlie we can adjust. Let's take them out for lunch today. We can park the bike here, for now, and hire a cab.'

'That's not required. I have my car. I'll drive Ma and Baba back home, and then we can join you,' Presha said with a tinge of innocence on her face. I loved her expressions and was getting attracted towards her.

'You guys can join us at the *Hyatt*. We can order lunch in my room,' I said.

'Fine, we'll be there within an hour,' Presha was enthused with the idea.

Presha and Ananya reached the *Hyatt* at around 2:30 p.m. Ananya was busy checking out books displayed in the lounge. Presha called up my room from the desk, and within no time, I was in the lobby to receive them. Presha walked towards me, but, at first glance, I was unable to recognize her.

13

She was in western attire; her face looked much better in the natural glow of her skin than when I first saw her on the stage with make-up. She looked a cool chic. For a moment, I was staggered to see her in a new avatar.

I knew I was getting charmed by Presha. Being fully aware of the sensitivity of the relationship with her and her family values, I would have dreaded to look at Presha in any other way except my buddy's cousin.

'Hey, Adie,' Presha said, looking into my eyes.

'Hello Presha, where's Ananya?' I said, stealing my eyes.

'Right there, she's a book lover,' Presha said, pointing towards Ananya. When Ananya saw me standing with Presha, she scampered towards us.

'Are you not fond of books?' I asked Presha, trying to sound formal.

'I find life is the most interesting book, and I prefer to read it rather than exploring some printed pages. What do you think?' Presha said, with tilted eyes.

'Dada, she's bluffing. Presha is a scholar and genius with numbers,' Ananya interrupted before Presha could say anything.

My brows were arched but within me, I wasn't convinced of what I heard. I was finding more of sex power in her rather than any brain power. Sure, she wasn't gorgeous, but indubitably she had a seductive appeal.

'Impressive!' I said, smiling at Ananya.

'Don't say anything unless you are convinced. Your words and your body speak different languages, which shows your confusion,' Presha said, staring at me.

'She's a trained micro expression reader. It's impossible to deceive her,' Ananya smirked.

I was abysmally embarrassed and frightened; what if she turns out to be a telepath as well, I wouldn't be able to show my face to Charlie.

Challenged by the situation, I became too audacious and said, 'Presha, even I like to be straight with people; but I was trying to maintain my decency by not telling you that your muliebrity seems to empower your intellect. You look more of a model than a scholar.'

'Adie, I'm knocked out. If a handsome man like you compliments a female like the way you did; I feel by now she should be meeting the God. You must be finding me tenacious; I'm still standing in front of you. But believe me, I'm melting like butter.'

I realized Presha respected no boundaries when she was charged. She made a monkey of me in front of Ananya, so avoiding any further discomfit I remarked, 'You are a dangerous girl. My apologies if I have hurt you in any way. But for now, let's go to my room and order some food; Charlie is ready to eat a horse.'

I must confess it was now difficult for me to take my eyes off Presha. She had a charismatic aura. She might not be the most beautiful woman in this world, but she sufficed to turn anyone crazy once you interacted with her.

We moved towards the elevators on the right. I entered the whisking box after the girls, behind Presha. The scent of her spray was turning me as mad as a hatter. In fact, everything about her looked bewitching now. I can call it love on the first day; I know it would have been difficult for me to get involved in love at first sight; my perspicacious brain takes its own time, and I always considered that it controlled my heart.

When we entered the room, Charlie was already ordering the food, and I heard him order two chicken dishes.

'Two! It's true, I'm famishing but don't consider my belly a gorge,' I was trying to protect my image with Presha. She shouldn't envisage me, gluttony.

'It's for Presha as well. She's also in love with non-vegetarian food, especially, chicken.'

'You seem to be quite a rebel, 'I said, looking at Presha.

'It's up to you to call me anything, but I believe that you get only one life; you should lead it the way you like it.'

I was already wounded; there was no need for her to bombard me with her philosophies.

My wicked mind was pondering on how to turn away Charlie and Ananya from this place; I wanted to be alone with Presha, I was getting too curious to know more about her. I felt, even Presha wanted to be left alone with me for some time.

At times destiny favors you. 'I have to be back by five o'clock for coaching classes. I can't afford to miss it, and neither can I reach late. Hurry up! Presha, you need to finish eating fast,' Ananya said.

'Ananya, I don't know when we are going to meet next. Spend some more time here; enjoy your food and afterward, Charlie can drop you on the bike.'

'Perfect!' Ananya said. It sounded an ideal solution to everyone's desires.

'Sure, and Presha can accompany you for shopping,' Charlie said acting like an indiscreet bro.

The whole room was enthused by smiles.

Finally, we two were alone.

* * * * *

I looked at Presha, her lips were preparing to make a movement. 'I can't imagine that you are interested in going to shopping with me. It'll be a waste of time,' remarked Presha.

'In fact, I want to. I desire to know more about you; and shopping with you, can give me a great opportunity,' I was trying to be candid with her before she finds out something using her skills or sixth sense. By then, I was damn scared of interacting with her.

'I'm sure you'll like to find something positive about me. I'm very impatient when I accompany someone for shopping.'

'Strange! It's the first time I have heard a female saying she doesn't like shopping.'

'You heard it wrong; I said, I don't like accompanying someone for shopping. I can shop for countless hours, but I don't prefer anyone to be with me in my extravaganza.

'You can go shopping tomorrow with Charlie. Come on, today I'll take you to places where you can know real Presha.'

'Why are you scaring me every time? I'm getting skeptical about your intentions. You are crazy...'

'If you have gut of a man, follow me....'

Presha was quite often slaughtering my ego, which made me ill at ease, but to my surprise, I wasn't grouchy. I was flowing with her.

She took me to *Roxy*, a nightclub in *The Park Hotel*. I had been to the place twice earlier with college friends. It's a cavernous bar with a retro glam look. It's a classy place, but it was an albatross on our pockets at that time.

Presha was right, I knew her better now– she was flamboyant, bizarre and fun loving person. I found her like my mirror image, and as we were humans and not magnets like poles were attracting each other.

By dim met, I was mind boggled by Presha. She was a lot more demented, than what I had anticipated. She sent a text to Ananya, "I'm with Adie at *Roxy*, and we won't be able to take calls henceforth. Handle everyone at home," and she switched off our mobiles.

'What Charlie's going to think about me?' I yelled at Presha.

'Chill! Charlie won't have the time to think over, like you. He'll be busy, pacifying Ma and Baba. Don't you worry, he's an expert. I keep challenging his skills every now and then.

'So, where do we start from, I think beer should be okay with me. What about you?' Presha said with a finger-patting her lip. Her bold expressions reflected as if she was doing all the noble things.

'And where's the end going to be?' I asked her sardonically.

'Till they throw us out of this place, and you take me to your hotel,' she grinned.

'Gauche! It's not possible.' I said sternly. I would have been gaga about it if she wasn't Charlie's cousin.

'Adie, once I have decided to do it, I'm anyways going to accomplish it. You are free to walk out of this place. I'll text Charlie to pick me up and drop me at your hotel. I'm not piling up on you; it's just that I haven't made any alternate arrangements.'

'Presha, you are making me helpless.'

'Um... lots of people have praised me for my capabilities.'

I don't know what was happening to me, I was mesmerized or, may be, I was enjoying every bit of her.

'A beer for me,' I sounded like a surrendered man.

'Two Stellar Artois,' Presha told the bartender.

The staff there was familiar and friendly with Presha. She seemed to be frequently flocking the place.

Nowhere in our interaction, I felt that she had crossed the limits of decency. She was obstinate at times. Okay! Every time. Otherwise, she was a well-balanced girl.

As the evening progressed, I realized I was the one doing all the talking and she kept gazing at my face, processing my words and expressions. She was also preoccupied with her drinks; next to the beer it was Caipiroska, vodka.... She was a tippler. I was indulging in Malbec, a red wine. With every glass going down, I was invigorated and enunciated, more than even what was required. Presha was watching me carefully, even in the drunken state; leaning back in her stool, she would have screened my real self.

Ten o'clock: I was exhausted. Presha ordered her supposedly last drink. At this time, genuinely, she was in a state to be thrown out. She swigged her glass till the last drop, but still she was sucking it to find a droplet of the vodka smearing the sides of the glass.

I could still manage myself better. I knew it was the time to go back as Presha was inebriated, and should be taken back before it gets embarrassing. I extended her a hand, and as she was climbing down the stool, she plummeted on me. I raised her and toted her to the couch at the back of the bar area.

I had no choice but to call up Charlie to tell him the state of affairs.

'Hi, Charlie,' I said in a faint voice.

'Are you okay?' Charlie was anxious.

'What would happen to me?' I said, mustering my energy.

'No, nothing, Presha's with you, is it?' asked poor Charlie, holding his breath.

I was perplexed to find Charlie worried about me rather than Presha.

'I know she's a gadfly, and this time, you are the sucker punch.' Charlie was being too honest.

'No, she's quite forthright. She told me about the outcome when we started the evening.

'Tell me what needs to be done now, she's blacked out.

'If you find it okay, I can drop her at home.'

'Don't even think of getting her here; take her to your hotel.

'Once there, gimme a call. I want to meet you.'

'Okay, bye.'

I took out the car keys and parking token from her handbag. Thank God! I was able to locate them easily in the back pocket of her bag. I took assistance from the staff out there, schlepped Presha to the car's back seat. I slid behind the wheel, turned around to look at Presha, who lay unconscious with a half smile, and a feeling of gratification, on her face.

Finally, I drove her to my hotel.

The scene was quite awkward; Presha in my arms, Akanksha, and a few pals checking in at the reception. I was so prominent; anyone would have turned around to give me a look.

Akanksha gave me an evil eye, I smiled wryly, and she looked at me with disgust, as if carrying an insentient girl is a crime. I scurried towards the elevator ignoring everyone out there. I dashed inside, relieved to find it vacant.

I opened the door of my room and laid her on the neatly made bed.

I was shocked at my behavior. There would be countless instances when I had slept with my shoes on; if I was tired and I lay on the bed, I was off in a nanosecond. But that day I took out Presha's high heeled sandals, heavy funky Jewelry, and jacket, to make her comfortable. She was wearing a black spaghetti looking all the more attractive. It was the time when my eyes were dancing, on her to find her swanky. I saw the tattoos on her inner bicep and neck. The bicep tattoo said, *Love is Faith*. It would have been a painful experience to get them pierced, but the girl seemed willing to go several miles to satisfy her whims. I was fascinated by the zing in her.

As decided, I called up Charlie and he asked me to meet him at the coffee house. I was apprehensive about his reaction; I was also responsible for the day's happenings. I could have taken an assertive stand and said, *no* to her, but instead, I moved with her. Anyways, I mustered the courage to face him.

There came Charlie, as expected a little panicked.

'How's Presha?' Charlie asked with standing creases between his eyebrows.

'She's absolutely fine; sleeping. I have made her comfortable, so she should be okay,' I said. But Charlie's eyes were wide open with several questions floating in them. I could see he was curious to talk to me.

'Adie, you are entering into a mess. Why did you go with her?'

'She didn't give me any choice.'

'You could have called me before venturing with her.'

'Oh God! Now this is heights, Charlie. You know I never ask anyone for my decisions.'

'But she's my cousin; at least, this should have been enough to put the brakes on you.'

'What's your problem? I liked her and I wanted to spend some time with her, that's it.'

'This is my problem; it's not as cool as you are sounding. Presha is a very emotional girl and I have never seen her falling for any guy like the way she's going for you.

'I know her, it's something much more severe than liking, and I know you as well, you always want to be a free bird. Though, I feel, you are also getting inclined towards her, but beyond that, I'm not sure.'

'You know me right, I'm fascinated by her, but beyond that, I haven't got anything on my mind.'

'Fabulous! At least, now I know, you aren't going to be the trouble.'

'You are telling me that she's serious about me, and if, I also get inclined towards her, it would be a problem!

'No, no, come again! Are you saying if I'm interested in a relationship with Presha, it's a trouble!

'She's your sister… damn it! You aren't concerned about her feelings.' I said, frowning.

'Wait! Listen, Adie, it's serious. Presha belongs to a traditional family; and her parents, would go to any extent to ensure she marries a Bengali Brahmin,' Charlie said with a stern face.

'Oh! Presha is the outcome of tradition.'

'Nope. They have given her the full liberty to live her life in her own way, but this thing is writing on the wall.'

'How do you think Presha would react if her folks resist to our relationship?'

'She'll rebel. But she's mawkish too; she loves her parents immensely, is also equally true.'

'Are you saying she'll neither leave her parents nor me, she'll sacrifice her life waiting for me? No, no, she's no nitwit!'

'She'll not cease now, maybe after some time she'll have qualms.'

'Sorry, Charlie, I don't buy this. You are anticipating too much.'

'Adie, she's my sister and very dear to me. I would like her to be the happiest person on this earth.

'The truth is, you are also my friend and I can't see you in a fix as well. Presha is pig-headed so she can create a lot of troubles in your life. You too are an obstinate person; I don't see it working either way.'

'Charlie, you don't sound convincing.'

'I'm saying it in the best interest of both of you.'

'You are too late. I love her,' I said it from the subconsciousness, even till then my conscious mind hadn't processed it yet.

'Hurry up! Finish your coffee fast. Presha is alone, I need to go,'

'What are you up to, Adie?' Charlie said in a stew.

'I promise I'll never hurt you,' I said with a broad smile; and Presha, radiating on my face.

'Good night, Charlie.'

'BTW, I'm taking back Presha's car. It'll help me to create a story.

'Hope you are joining us for the meet tomorrow,' Charlie said like a lost man.

'Ridiculous! Of course, I'll be there.' I remarked.

'Not sure!' Charlie felt his hands tied and he moved out.

Charlie knew me better than anyone else. He was sure that no one would be able to change our resolution. He felt powerless. The only option was to convince Ma and Baba, which was easier, said than done.

I came back to my room, convinced that Presha is my future. I was also conscious of Charlie's sentiments, and in no way, I was going to hurt him. I loved challenges, so I wasn't feeling any butterflies in my stomach. I was exuberant about the outcome.

It was like asking too much for me to sleep on the couch. I was a comme il faut, but by no means an Absolute Being. I preferred to be a human being; life was comfortable that way. I decided to share the bed with Presha. I lay beside her, resisting myself, to look at her. I didn't know when her face stupefied me; her intense expressions could flummox anyone. I was trying to read her as she lay there in a drunken stupor; she looked like an open book with a few hidden pages. With every passing moment, I could feel a notion descending inside me that life would be impossible without her. I didn't realize when sleep crept into my eyes hardly making any noise.

I woke up by the quiver in the bed. It was Presha squirming. It was time to finish her carouse and face the life with the sunrise.

Before Presha was up, I ordered a black coffee for her. I could feel the transformation in me, from a reckless guy to a responsible man.

There was a knock at the door; it was a room boy. He set the coffee on the table, and his eyes surreptitiously looked for Presha. No wonder! The way I scampered into the hotel last night, carrying inebriated Presha in my hands, caught everyone's attention and curiosity.

As soon as he moved out, Presha opened her eyes and stared at me.

'Do you love me? I have given you the night to think about it,' she said.

'Only this much, now I can't think of a life without you,' I replied in a similar tone.

'Terrific! You are honest, this time.

'So what do you plan now?' Presha said shrugging her shoulders.

'Plan? I want to have a relationship with you.'

'Adie, don't you think you are a bit slow?

'I'm asking you, how do you plan to have a relationship?'

'You go home, and inform your parents about our decision. After reunion party, I'll come to your place and formally ask for your hand from your Baba.'

'And you think, Baba will be exhilarated, and he'll hug me tightly.

'Damn it! I can't even think of doing anything idiotic like facing him before we marry.

'He's never going to agree and I'm not going to stop. And nor do I want to offend him by not listening to him.'

'Hold on! You are driving me crazy, Presha!

'What do you intend to do?'

'I don't wanna give him a chance to speak. Let's start our romantic odyssey.'

'What? I came here for a reunion meet. Charlie and everyone else will be waiting for me.

'Gimme a day. It's okay, even if you are planning to act crazy! Let me get the reservations for tomorrow,' I nodded my head as if I was justifying my words.

'Hey, Adie, there has to be some spice in life. Just imagine Charlie's face when he'll come to know that you have left for Delhi with me on his Hyosung!'

'You are nuts Presha!

'But, but this sounds interesting,' I was enthused.

Nobody would have expected such an irresponsible and kiddish behavior from me. The truth of the moment was, everything suggested by Presha was pounding my heart and bringing me closer to myself. I was always passionate about life with no holds barred. Life was offering me the chance.

My phone buzzed, and it was Charlie's name flashing on the screen.

'Hey buddy, good morning,' I said in a thrilled voice.

'Where are you?'

'I'm just moving out to drop Presha to her friend's place.'

'Adie, we are already late. Everyone would have reached by now.'

'No worries, I'll be there in half an hour,' I hung up the phone.

I called up a cab to carry my luggage. On the way to Delhi, I air booked the luggage. When I came out of the building, Presha was sitting on the bike waiting for me. I looked at her and took a deep breath. I could feel the freshness permeating within me. I waved at her and she kick started the bike. I jumped in the back seat as if I had surrendered my life to her. I was ready to follow her anywhere.

I was pillion riding with a girl for the first time. I wasn't sure how to carry myself. I don't know what happened to me that I didn't follow my natural self. I hugged her tightly with my torso pressing her back.

The slight twist in her body showed me that she wasn't too comfortable with my intimacy. I realized the presence of an Indian male in me, as I was happy at traditional tinge in Presha. I withdrew myself a bit to make her comfortable.

Before we could discern, we were communicating telepathically, for more than an hour. We heaved euphoric sighs in between as an acknowledgment of our emotions.

Presha was quite a good driver. She drove 100 miles non-stop, and then she halted at a roadside tea stall. I wondered if she would have tea at that place.

'A dash of milk,' I said, without asking Presha, what was she up to?

Presha got down off the bike, took off her helmet; her hair, which she had tied in a bun avalanched on her shoulders, tempting me to take a plunge.

'A cigarette, and a cup of tea with a little milk,' she said to the boy there who seemed stunned by her.

'Yes, ma'am.'

Putting the cigarette in her mouth, she asked the guy to light the butt. He did as told, and the smile on the boy's face reflected satisfaction on his accomplishment.

I was gazing at her from my pillion seat. Presha was a damn cool girl, or at least, she projected so.

She came towards me and said, 'Do you mind a puff?'

'No thanks, I don't smoke.'

'Great! Anyways, it's injurious to your health.

'Whenever, I feel stressed out, I smoke; it soothes your nerves,' Presha remarked.

'Hmm...

'Has driving stressed you?' I knew it was dumb on my part to ask such a ridiculous question, but then I wasn't an extrovert like Presha and desired if she could share her heart with me.

'Shut up! It's just I have never been away from Ma and Baba; coming this far off, reminiscence me of them. They love me a lot and so do I.'

I wanted to tell her that her love was quite evident from her act of eloping with a guy whom she had met just a day back. But, as I said I wasn't like Presha, so I preferred to be quiet. However, I got a little jittery with her vacillating mind.

'Do you plan to go back?' I said, befuddled on her intent.

'Nope. I wouldn't have stopped here if I wished so.'

She puffed, and said with a grinning face, 'Nicotine will help me to manage this transition. Everyone needs to grow up one day.'

I only wanted to squeak *Moppet*, but then, all the more I was falling in love with her for her innocence, and obstinate love.

My hand slid on her cheek, her touch was magical. Presha was unperturbed.

'Let's go,' I said, taking the keys from her hand.

Presha sat at the back with her arms lightly embracing my waist. There was a deafening silence for a while,

'This thing called love I just can't handle it

'This thing called love I must get round to it

'I ain't ready

'Crazy little thing called love......,' Presha started singing in her not so melodious voice.

I was enjoying every moment. She was ecstatic at times; and tranquil in between, as if she was giving herself some rest.

I drove quietly for four hours, sensing her mood swings; and listened to the same lyrics in a rather dissonant voice.

I stopped the bike near the city of Gaya, for lunch. It was again a countryside food joint. While we were waiting for the food, I started humming.

'Adie, what's that?' Presha said with a face beaming with surprise.

'This thing called love I just cann't handle it

'this thing called love I must get round to it

'I ain't ready

'Crazy little thing called love......,' I crooned.

'You are toooo....good! Breathtaking voice! I never knew, you too are a singer.

'Why didn't you sing with me when I was running through the song?'

'I'm not a professional singer,' before I could complete, Presha jumped in between.

'But, anyways, you could have tried it with me; you also, sing so well,' said Presha, shrugging her shoulders and her hands popped out.

'I know, but it wasn't possible for me to stoop down to your level. You were raucous.' Presha was stunned to hear me.

'Presha, you know the problem is, no one can lie to you,' I said, pampering her.

'You have a melodious voice, Adie. You can expose yourself.

'And I'm not going to stop singing. I love it, and who cares what people say; even if you are one of them,' said Presha, undisturbed, with a smiling face.

I would be candid; my ego was hurt– the way she gave a damn to me. Anyways, I liked her candor and freewheeling attitude.

'I love you the way you are, Nightingale. I hope you don't mind that name.'

'I know you are not too upright. But then, it's the most beautiful name I could have even thought of,' Presha said holding my hand. The warmth of her touch and stars in her eyes tickled me to death. I kissed her hand.

We had lunch, and we moved out to resume our journey.

It seemed as if we had known each other for ages. It's just that vicious circle of life and death had parted us for some time.

I was a pillion rider this time. Unconsciously, I put my arms around her waist and rested my head on her back. Soon I realized it and was withdrawing myself back when she held my hands and drew them closer to her body. I was melting in her warmth.

In no time, Presha started reciting her memoir. Her tales were horrifying me. She was a ruthless tomboy in her childhood.

Once she was writing her exam, she got confused about a question. She asked the guy sitting next to her for help. He pointed towards the professor and showed his inability to extend a helping hand to her. The examiner was on vigilance and the moment he turned his back, Presha stood up from her chair; snatched the answer sheet from the boy to give it back to him, only after, validating her concern, or simply, after copying.

She was incessant on how justified her conduct was, and what harm can weaklings cause to humanity. On my side, I was appalled; fell short of words to react, so preferred to be a good listener. I could comprehend that she was erratic, and she could go to a great extent to justify her point of view.

I was feeling all the more strongly for her after listening to her eccentricity. She was a free bird like me, impossible to cage.

'Adie, you aren't saying anything,' said Presha, realizing my silence, but only after two hours.

'What to say, I was never as heroic as you were.

'I studied what I wanted to; I always had a lifestyle of my choice; I started drinking in the final year of engineering; I mean I always took independent decisions for myself. But nowhere on par with you or your independence: which seems is beyond boundaries. You can poach on anyone's freedom for your liberty.'

'Oh God! It's not that serious.

'Chill!'

'No, I genuinely feel I can learn a lot from you, like, new dimensions of independence.'

'Good, I can motivate you.'

Thank God! She wasn't looking at my face. But I was sure, she knew I made fun of her.

* * * * *

Around midnight, we were half way through; we decided to stop at a nearby hotel. I switched on my cell as soon as I entered the room. It was time to lend an ear to my consciousness, which was nagging me to call Charlie. Fingers pressed his name with a thumping heart. There was silence on the other end.

'Hey! Charlie, say something buddy. Your silence is shattering.'

'How's Presha?'

'Good.'

'Where are you?'

'Varanasi.'

'What the hell are you doing there?'

'We are traveling by your bike.'

'It's crazy!'

'No, it's thrilling. Trust me.'

'Silly! What you guys are up to?'

'I thought you would have guessed it by now. She's going to Singapore with me. We have planned to stay together for life.'

'What? Are you out of your mind? It's not feasible.'

'Charlie, no one can stop us now. We have already taken a decision,' I said, with firmness; to thrash, if any hope that was still left with Charlie.

'Leave aside everything, but what about Presha's parents?'

'Convince them; I know two of us are precious to you, so give some efforts to make our life happy. Anyways, Presha told me that she has trained you enough to handle them.'

'Presha, Presha, Presha. Adie, you have gone crazy. This girl is nuts.'

'Charlie, she's my life now.' I could imagine there, Charlie with his hands clenched and lips twisted.

I could hear, Charlie inhale- exhale for some time, and then he said, 'I pray both of you keep your plans even after reaching Delhi.

'Adie, please ensure marriage is solemnized in a traditional way. As is, it's going to be difficult for Ma and Baba to digest this news. At least, try to give them some solace they deserve.'

'You sound disturbed, buddy.'

'Uh! There's nothing to be ecstatic about. You two have sought a self-obsessed path; but Adie, unfortunately, life is not only about self. Hopefully, you'll understand it one day,' agony in Charlie's voice hammered my heart.

'Bro, it was impossible for me to imagine a life sans Presha. Never before had I felt so deeply the puissance of someone.'

'I can imagine. Two tomfools are bound to think that way.'

'You don't trust us.'

'Not a pinch. I know you two very well.

'Give me a buzz when you reach home, and best of luck for your life!

'You too are and will always remain dear to me. Bye.'

'Bye.'

I was almost in tears when I hung up the phone. I questioned myself, "Is it worthwhile– slaughtering sentiments of people who are so dear to us?" My inner voice dragged me to Presha and a sound echoed in my ears– "Everything is justified if you believe in it."

Presha didn't show any interest in my conversation with Charlie. It seemed she was evading it. She could see the distress on my face, so she tried to assuage it with a kiss. Not a bad deal.

I was about to reciprocate her passion, but there was a gong at the door. It was the waiter, with specially made food at our request at the wee hours. This is the beauty of downtown hotels in our country; they treat their guests as God.

After dinner, Presha desired to get drunk. She was a big tanker, any time of the day or night she was ever ready for drinks. I wasn't gung-ho on her ambitions; I decided to take some rest, as after a few hours we had to resume the thrilling journey planned by Presha. Sense prevailed on my Nightingale and she followed the suit. But for some time I heard her humming 'Crazy little thing called love.....,' before I went to sleep.

When I woke up in the morning, it was eight o'clock. Presha was asleep. Hair strands falling on her face looked so beautiful. I wished I could have gazed her for hours, but my biological clock pushed me to the washroom.

Presha was watching TV when I came out. It looked to me as if she was trying to find out if her Baba had issued a search warrant for her.

'Good Morning,' Presha said with a bright face.

'Good Morning; Nightingale, you sing horribly. Do you often try it?' I said as if it was something like a stone burdening my head, and I wanted to take it off as soon as possible.

'But my voice had a lullaby magic on you.'

'I didn't have any choice but to wander in dreamland, reality was too dreadful.'

'Do you mean to say I'm dreadful? Crazy!'

'You should have known countless guys hitting on me.'

'I could see that in your college. I thought you were different. You are a typical girl who likes boys chasing you.'

'You are right; I'm a straight girl if you meant that.'

'Okay, Miss Perfect. Are you ready to make a move?'

'You guys have a bad habit of living your own life, but not giving any space to others.'

'Oh ho! What happened now?'

'I need to go for ablutions.'

'Go. Hurry up!'

Presha was set in ten minutes, and we were out to restart our journey. She sat on the bike embracing me tightly. The touch of her aesthetically crafted delicate and soft fingers; her fast paced rhythmic breathing was turning me crazy. I had to, in between, bring myself back from the wonderland to the road leading us to my home.

We two were fired up throughout our journey; whether it was chatting, singing, lunatic moves of our bike, stress busters of Presha; the bliss of everything were enchanting our hearts.

Presha was totally unfazed by how my parents would react to our gesture. She asked me to buy vodka and chicken kebabs as soon as we entered the borders of Delhi, my homeland. Unlike myself, I was behaving more responsibly; it could be the reaction of sweet spot I was put in by the time. I knew my parents were open-minded, and they had given me all the liberty in life, but, but still I wanted to be mature this time. Presha supported my viewpoint, she refrained herself from any more fantasies till we reached home.

Chapter 3

Before I pressed the doorbell, Muma opened the door. Since I got late, the anxiety had taken her into custody. I hugged her, and she kissed me on the forehead with her quintessential smile. This is how she handled my tantrums, with love and patience.

'You have been in India for four days now. Were you not eager to meet me any time? Adie, you have really grown big, or now, there's someone else in your life who has taken the priority,' Muma said, mockingly, as I had always been piqued by this discussion.

It reminded me of Presha who was incidentally hidden behind me. I moved sideways and said, pointing at Presha, 'Muma, this is Presha. She is Charlie's Cousin and...'

'And the one who has become your priority now,' Muma said cuddling Presha.

'Hello Aunty,' Presha said, embracing Muma with equal warmth.

'Muma, Charlie took me to her dance performance and after that, everything for me has been moving around Presha; I haven't even attended the reunion meet.'

'Fabulous! Much better reaction than what I had ever expected from you.

'Did you tell Presha that you were never a romantic guy, and there's some magic she has played on you.'

'I can vouch for it, he's a bore. The other day he found me so awful that he fell asleep while I was awake,' Muma was taken aback by Presha's remark.

'Where are you coming from?'

'Kolkata.'

'Oh! I never realized, planes from Kolkata have started halting in between for a night,' Muma said as if to rebuff what I told her.

'No, we have come by bike.'

'It's turning insane,' Muma said, pointing towards Presha, asking her to get inside.

We sat in the living room. Incongruous to Muma's disposition, she was looking at Presha with oblique eyes. Perhaps, what I told had created suspicions in her mind about the sagacity of Presha. She knew me well to realize that I wouldn't have architected our journey in that elegant manner.

'So, Presha is an adventurous girl,' Muma said, trying to break the silence echoing in the room.

'No, Auntie, I just do whatever I want to.'

'Muma, Presha wanted to leave Kolkata as soon as possible. She didn't want her folks to know about it, especially, Ma and Baba.'

'And you supported her cause!' Muma asked, raising a concern about my mental stability.

'Anyways, we had taken a decision about our life. In spite of it, I told her I would talk to her parents, but she was sure about their resentment, so she avoided confronting them.

'I feel it's her life, and she has every right to take her own decisions.'

Presha seemed indifferent about our discussion. Her eyes roved over the house.

'Do you want anything Presha?' I said.

'Yeah, tell me, where your room is? I'm tired, I want to relax.

'Meanwhile, if you can order chicken kebabs and a bottle of vodka.'

Muma looked at me in astonishment. No wonder, Presha's level of freedom was several folds higher than mine.

'Sure, Presha I'll show you the guest room. Till then, Adie can order your desired food,' Muma said. I could see the impatience in Muma's tone which I had never felt earlier.

I placed the order at *24X7 kitchen*, and ad interim, Muma took Presha in the guest room. She took more time to come out than I had even anticipated. Presha asked her for a night dress and she was trying to find one for her.

After dropping a nightgown with Presha, Muma rushed back to me in the living room.

'Adie, have you gone nuts?'

'Muma, what's happened to you?'

'You have always given me my space, then what's the problem now?'

'Adie, you are an intelligent adult so there's no question of interfering in your life.

'But this time, I feel you don't even realize what you are getting into. It's a question of your life.

'I find Presha immature; she can't give you any stability.'

'Muma, anyways who wants stability? She's independent, brilliant with freshness of thoughts; I feel life can be exciting, with her.'

'You two are very similar. Imagine the state when one of you needs to be different to handle the situation. You two are headstrong, and your mindsets too seem to be synchronized.'

'Funny! You should be rather happy, we'll have fun flocking together,' I said, getting off the couch to attend the buzz at the door.

I heard Muma saying, 'Okay! Enjoy your dinner. I'll talk to you tomorrow,' and she moved to her room.

It was a delivery boy at the door. The tantalizing aroma of kebabs made me scuttle to my room to pick up bottles of vodka and red wine, and within a nanosecond, I was knocking at the room of Presha.

'Please come in.'

'Yummy! The food is here,' I said, placing the stuff on the table.

I raised my head, and I burst into laughter to find Presha looking like a buffoon in Muma's oversized gown. But, again, the hair strands falling on her face were enough to pummel my heart mercilessly. Taking my eyes off her, I opened the vodka and poured it into the glasses lying in the room. I knew Presha was feeling anxious, she required alcohol to soothe her nerves rather than to party.

Helping her to relax and feel better, I put on the song which she hummed to maraud the peace throughout the journey, "Crazy little thing called love......".

There was a smile on Presha's face, and I knew just to avoid an eye contact she was glued to BBC News. I was apprehensive if she would have ever taken any interest in what's happening around the world, as with her mindset, I feel, her life always would have been the most happening; at least, enough to keep her involved in herself.

'Hey, Presha! What's going on in your mind?'

'What should I do next?'

'Off course, marry me and then we are off to Singapore.'

'I want to call Ma and Baba for the marriage.'

'I don't think even Muma is going to let it happen without them.'

'No, I'll talk to them myself.'

'Your, wish!'

'Then, I was thinking, what am I going to do in Singapore?'

'Do whatever you want.'

'I don't have an iota of doubt that I'll do something which I don't want to do. I'm exploring what it will be that can interest me?'

'Presha, let's go step by step. First, let's get married and then we can think about other details.'

'No, I have decided to take a call today itself.'

'Okay, you decide. I'm tired; I'll go to my room.'

'Even, I 'm tired, but still, this is serious.'

"By Joe, she can't be inebriated so soon. But then she's always....."

'Fine, I'm here. Say, what's your plan like.'

'I'll like to complete my graduation. You are so educated; at least, I should be a graduate.'

'This is a great thought,' I said.

'I know you aren't lying this time,' Presha said with a wicked smile on her face.

"Oh shit! She's a pain when she starts dissecting your expressions."

'Next, I feel we should discuss our home. How many rooms do you have in your apartment?'

'It's a studio.'

'Never mind. But, is it spacious? I always dreamt of a hanging bed.'

'What???'

'Yes. I'm sure it'll be an awesome experience. You need to be closer to the moon to savor honey.'

'Anything else,' I was enjoying her exhilaration on our new beginning.

'Yes, of course!

'I want our house should have nature's bliss.'

'No Presha. Singapore is an expensive country. Right now we can't afford to own a big space there.'

'Uh-uh…

'Those tiny creatures don't require any space,' Presha said with the innocence of a child.

'Which type of creatures?'

'Birds, rabbits..'

'Presha, don't you think it will be a great idea if we get some space in a zoo. Wow! Anyways, we'll be always hanging in the air and closer to, not only the moon but the entire celestial world.

'I heard, after death you go to GOD, who's residing somewhere in that world,' I said, getting cramped with her ever increasing horrific hallucinations.

'I know you are acting mean. But for me, its like dream coming true if I spend my life closer to nature.'

'Anything else, you have on your splendid list?' Presha was looking so cute with her relentless prattling. I wished if she could go on like this.

My desire came true. She gabbled till dawn, I kept staring her with a glass of wine in hand. If God existed, he was fulfilling all my wishes at the moment.

We decided to take a nap for a few hours, who knew what lay in store for us.

As I was coming out of the guest room, I saw Muma in front of me going towards the kitchen, perhaps, to prepare bed tea.

'Good morning, Mom.'

'Good morning, Adie. Care for some tea.'

'No, thanks. I'll take a nap.' Muma was great; She had never questioned me about anything.

I had always appreciated Mom for giving me full space, even when I was a kid. But, candidly, I was embarrassed when she saw me coming out of the guest room.

'What about Presha?'

'She has gone to sleep just now. Moreover, she'll need a lemonade and not tea when she gets up,' I said, smirking.

'You kids are hopeless,' and two of us headed to our respective destinations.

It was around 3:00 p.m., I came out of my room. Muma was watching TV in the living room, and Papa was all wound up in the newspaper.

'Hi, Papa.'

'Hello sonny,' Papa said, hugging me tightly.

'How's life? Is anything worthwhile in the newspaper?'

'Son, it depends on you, what do you look for.

'Oh yeah, if you are yourself busy creating news; it's hard to find something worthwhile elsewhere.'

'Come on Dad! Wait. I will introduce you to Presha. Then we'll talk.'

'Your Mom has already spoken a lot about her. I'm sure she's unique.

'But I don't like the way you guys have worked out the things.'

'Adie, you should immediately call Charlie,' Muma told, looking a little worried.

'Oh Shit! I forgot to call him yesterday night.'

'He called up in the morning. He sounded perturbed. No wonder he would be,' Muma's annoyance was evident in her voice.

'I'm so sorry. I'm calling him right away.'

Moving towards my room, I called him,' Sorry buddy. Presha got involved in drinks and then we both were discussing our future; didn't realize when the sun was above our heads. My mistake, I completely missed out to call you.'

'Adie, I'm telling you, you are going to ruin yourself with her. Two of you are mindless.

'For God sake, listen to me.'

'Charlie, now I can't take anything against Presha. I don't mind whatever you tell me, but please don't say it for Presha.'

'Damn it! She's my sister. I want to protect both of you.'

'She's my life now. Stop being a philanthropist, and be happy with what's happening.'

'Inform Presha's Ma Baba that we are getting married tomorrow; anyways, you have to be here for the marriage.'

'Ma and Baba are also coming.'

'Cool!

'How did it happen?'

'Life's not going to stop if two insane drunkards have decided to jeopardize their lives,' Charlie sounded helpless.

'Your Mom spoke to Ma and Baba, and convinced them to attend the wedding.'

'Didn't they throw any tantrums? I'm sure they would have cursed me.'

'They were numb; tears were rolling down their tired eyes. You guys have left them handcuffed.'

'Presha will be excited to know they're coming. She needs to know the news.

'So let's meet tomorrow. Bye buddy,' I said focusing on the outcome and ignoring the agony we had caused to anyone.

'Good luck! Bye,' Charlie hung up the phone, and I rushed to Presha's room. Presha was in slumber. I called her name several times, but she didn't even move. She was sleeping so peacefully, I didn't want to disturb her, but I was so excited for her. I was too eager to share the news with her.

I went to the kitchen, prepared two cups of black coffee; I knew she would require it to get back to consciousness. I placed the cups on the tray; I was holding a tray for the first time in my life– realized lifting dumbbells, is quite easier than carrying a tray in a formal fashion. My parents were slyly watching my every move with a kind of strange satisfaction on their faces. I entered the guest room, setting the tray with a slight thud on the side table. I sat quietly beside Presha, observing her keenly. Her expressions were erratic. It seemed a lot was happening in her subconsciousness. She looked furious at times; she was smiling in between as if everyone had bowed down to her decisions; then, intermittently there were flashes of disappointment. Her countenance was going down my line, and I sat there for almost half an hour following her, before I realized the reason I was there for. If a Psychiatrist had seen me in that state, I would have for sure been declared as a lunatic. I had no choice but to shake her, calling her name aloud. She opened her eyes in a state of shock.

'What happened? Is everything okay?' Presha stared at me.

'It's just 4:00 p.m., and I have some news for you.'

'I hope it's good,' Presha said, crossing her fingers.

'We're getting married tomorrow, and guess what?'

'What??' Presha said, throwing her arms.

'Your Ma and Baba are coming here for the wedding.'

'Wow! So they are okay with my act.'

'I don't know, but they are going to be here tomorrow.'

Presha seemed least interested in knowing, how it happened.

'Let's go shopping,' Presha said.

'You were never interested in shopping with someone.'

'Yes, but I'm also not interested in becoming the bride in an unusual attire– three days old white shirt turned black due to dust, and a stinky pair of jeans.'

'You have a valid point. Let's go.'

* * * * *

'Muma, we are going out for shopping. Presha can also buy her wedding dress.'

'Wait, Adie!'

'What, Muma?'

'Try buying some traditional dress.'

'We'll see.'

I took Presha to the *South-Ex* market for shopping casual wears. She wanted to be herself on our wedding day, not a lot different. We decided to go to *Ritu Kumar, Greater Kailash,* for buying her wedding attire.

She selected an aqua blue spaghetti strap gown for the ceremony. I knew she would have to sit on the ground for the rituals and the dress might not be too comfortable for the purpose, but then, it was her wish.

We came back around midnight. By the time, my parents had arranged everything for the marriage. Our family priest was informed, the first family and closest friends were invited, and an event manager was also appointed. Next, it was to hang fire till the sunrise, and my life would change after that. I had never imagined my life would be fast forwarded within a week's time.

We decided to keep it a dry night and sleep early for the occasion. We slept at two o'clock in the morning; as Presha thought, we should, at least, initiate the celebrations with beer. Presha and I were enjoying every moment, but not sure about Muma and Papa. They seemed to have a mixed reaction.

2 Dec 2007 3:00 p.m.: Presha rushed at the beauty parlor booked by Mom, in anticipation. It was evening, and the ceremony's scheduled time was 7:00 p.m. I was dressed up in a black Armani suit bought for the reunion, but who knew it would be worn for a union. Without trying to sound cocky, I was looking debonair in black that day.

Around 5:00 p.m., Presha's Ma and Baba, along with Charlie arrived at our house. My parents were ecstatic to see them. I felt as if they had found some support, and they won't allow us to bully them anymore.

There arrived Presha in her flowing gown. She was looking sexy and gorgeous too. She was wearing light makeup; her skin was radiating, maybe with excitement.

Now it was the time of confrontation. I was eager to see how she handles her parents. As soon as she entered the room, she faced them as they were sitting in the living room. She rushed to embrace them, surprisingly with no sign of guilt or fear on her face. Her Ma rebuffed her hand; getting up from the couch, she said, 'How are you dressed, Presha?'

'Isn't it a nice gown? Even Adie liked it,' Presha said, and my Mom turned her face towards me in astonishment. She knew I was always my real self in any situation, and the fact was I was sensible. I slightly shook my head refuting it; the complete truth was I liked it, but she never asked about my opinion on whether to buy it or not. But, anyways, Ma was unconvinced by her justification.

'He's a guy, can't expect from him to have too much idea about traditions. We have given you liberty to lead your life in your own way doesn't imply that we haven't taught you to respect our culture.

'Take this saree; it's our ancestral wedding saree, being our only daughter you have a right to it,' Ma said, handing over the bright red sari with golden emboss on it. It was a picture perfect moment; Presha's face was screwed up, and for a change, her lips were tied as she avoided messing up with her mother. But for sure, she wanted to throw her newly acquired inheritance.

She didn't do anything crazy. She took the saree from Ma, went back to the parlor to change her getup. What came back, though, was not so bad looking Presha; but, undoubtedly, she was looking a lot better in her previous attire. But then, it was

Presha's turn to take a call and not mine. Somehow, I found my Mom very pleased when she saw Presha in bridal dress. I knew Mom had exquisite tastes; maybe, she was happy with the flexibility shown by Presha.

Marriage was solemnized. Our families seemed exhilarated. Contrary to what Presha thought her parents reactions would be, on her marrying a non-Bengali, they were pleased to meet me. I was Charlie's friend could have gone to my advantage, or perhaps, Presha's parents were relieved to find her settled somehow. It was a little scary, as it reflected their opinion about the darling daughter, and parents are the best judge.

Charlie made a smart move. He booked a suite in *Maurya Sheraton* for our wedding night. This was the sweetest gift he could have given us. These romantic people are truly amazing, I knew Charlie was one of them, but the extent stunned me. The room looked like a meadow of red and white colored lilies; I never knew lilies excited my Nightingale.

Piñata of rose petals was broken open with the opening of the door. Rose was the best gift I thought of presenting to Akanksha. She was gone, but the memories of my preferences still lingered in Charlie's mind.

As soon as Presha flicked the switch on the bedside table lamp, 'Crazy little thing called love......,' started playing somewhere in the room. I dreaded if it was Charlie, hidden in some corner trying to jazz up his skills. I was fortunate! It was a CD player connected to the lamp switch.

The mini bar was the most beautifully decorated area of the room. You think about a brand and it was there– Red wines, beer, vodka and several others to his credit. He seemed to have gone insane. Were we there to get inebriated? It was our wedding night, and our elevated passion sufficed to intoxicate us.

I was so damn true; her fragrance, velvety touch, perfectly contrived silhouette, dark tresses and to top it all, sparkles in her eyes drove me crazy as a loon. She was melting in me, and we were one enlightened soul. Never before, I had even imagined the esoteric power of love.

In the morning, Charlie was there to drive us back home. The house, which was bustling with people the previous night, was quiet. The guests were gone; Ma, Baba, and Charlie were the only visitors, ready with their baggage to leave for the airport.

Presha's parents seemed happy with the alliance which gave me the hebbie jebbies; there was something which I wasn't able to comprehend. Their daughter was so terror-stricken of their reaction about our relationship that she preferred to elope with me. However, they were delighted to meet me.

'Adie is a very decent guy. He'll take good care of you.

'You should try to be a sincere and dedicated wife,' Ma told Presha, hugging her.

'I know Ma, how to handle my relationships,' Presha said, sounding a little irked.

Chapter 4

At last, everything was settled; much better than expected. Now it was time to focus on going back to Singapore with Presha. I had already extended my leave by a week as I had anticipated getting dependent visa for Presha within a week.

Finally, Presha received her visa and we left for Singapore. I canceled the old lease and rented a new studio apartment as desired by Presha. Presha was busy converting our home into a zoo. She bought a pair of *Opaline love birds, one African Gray, two bunnies, and chins.* Still, she felt something was missing in her fantasy world.

On my end, I was trying to concentrate on my career as well. It was important to be doing well in the job if I had to afford Presha's extravaganza. I not only wanted to provide for it, but also desired to encourage it; as now, Presha's happiness was the motto of my life.

But working in the office was getting difficult for me. I always wanted to be back with her as soon as possible. I was losing the tag of the most hardworking employee. Anyways, I had learned the art of setting my priorities as per my wish–Presha.

Presha on her end was proving to be an awesome wife. She was too caring and sensitive. She had even learned to cook and was trying to venture into something different every day. In case, one of those days, God would have asked me that if I craved for something more in life, I would have told him that I wasn't aware of anything above him, and he was with me.

It was a dream life; and time was flying by, with every wink of an eye. We were completing a year of this magical time– our magnificent married life. A day after, it was our wedding anniversary, and two of us were working on our surprises. Presha and I didn't plan any formal honeymoon as it was against her philosophy of *living your entire life as a honeymoon*; for which she had made arrangements by dangling our bed. Crazy!

Six months back I had started planning for this day. To royally treat her flamboyancy, I had booked the whole *Macan Island*, 45 miles off the coast of West Java, Indonesia. For two nights, it cost me entire life savings, but, but for Presha, I could justify everything.

I had to inform Presha that we would leave for Indonesia the next day, preserving the sanctity of my surprise too. She was clearing the table after dinner when I approached her, 'Presha something urgent has come up. I need to fly to Indonesia tomorrow for two days for a conference.'

'Two days means you won't be here for our..., it's a problem. At least, you'll be back on the second day, before midnight.'

'Even that seems ambitious. I'll be back only by the third day.'

'Okay,' Presha looked at me with a blank face. I knew she was ready to burst any moment. Before our cute pets got the jitters of their generous hostess, I decided to come to the point.

'Nightingale, how can I not be with you on our big day? Why don't you accompany me on this trip?'

'So, you remember it.'

'Of course, I do!'

'Okay; but it seems not everything, just in bits and pieces,' Presha said with a wicked smile.

'No cutie, I remember everything,' I was mind boggled on what she was trying to hint at.

'How can you even remember the things which I haven't told you yet?' Presha was in the full mood to rag me.

'Like?' I said, innocently.

'Like I want you to cook for me on that day and baby feed me.'

'Presha, don't you find it kiddish!'

'Nope, it's absolutely okay; I want to explore some new shades of you,' Presha said cuddling on my back.

Loosening the grip I held her hands and twisted myself to face her,' Hold on! We'll walk your suggested path once we are done with our packing.'

'Packing! And that too with you.

'Good Night. I'll do it on the fly, tomorrow morning.

'BTW, I like your new Versace gray suit, black jeans........,' Presha suggested a long list and giggling she went off to bed.

It finally took me around two hours to pack two sky bags for two nights. I was aware of the reality of our honeymoon, so I had to take care of all the details.

Next day, 6:00 a.m.: When I opened my eyes, Presha was busy doing her daily chores. The first thing she used to do was feed our extended family; she next targeted her treadmill as she was a fitness freak. She was preparing the bed tea when I woke up.

'Good morning, Sweetie,' she greeted me with an everlasting smile.

'Good morning. Have you done your packing?'

'Yep,' she said, pointing to her traveler's bag.

'Is that all?'

'I suppose we are there only for two days.'

'Yeah. Right.'

Within an hour Presha was ready to make a move; waiting patiently for me to join her. She was agile and crisp in whatever she did, and I was always a laggard. Not my fault, the onus is on my mother. Muma had always taken care of everything so well that I was accustomed to an aristocratic lifestyle. Doing my own things bothered me. I persistently desired someone to hand hold me, or be a little more generous and do it for me. Contrary to what Presha might look like, she at times pampered me like my Muma. But it was selective; she did it when she wanted to do. Otherwise, I was left on my own.

1 Dec 2008, Monday 10:00 a.m.: We were on the flight, scheduled to fly in another twenty minutes. It was a ninety-minute flight; we landed at *Jakarta International Airport*. The taxi was ready to take us to *Ancol Marina*. I was sure, Presha would find out the truth as soon as we boarded a fast boat. However, she was apathetic about it, as if she was really accompanying me for a conference. It was unlike Presha. I wondered what had happened to her face reading skills!

I tried acting smart,'Wow! This time, it seems they have worked out a beautiful place.'

'Didn't you know the venue earlier?'

'I knew, but I never knew it'll be so picturesque.' It was hard to act dumb; still, everything was justified to impress Nightingale.

'What time is your session today?' Presha said.

'5:00-7:00 p.m.'

'Oh good! You can join me in the bar once you are done. Tell me, Adie, what's so special about bars.'

'You can go there at any time of the day,' I said, raising my hands.

'It's not so funny. The Bar is our identity,' she frowned at me.

'Come on! It can be yours, but not mine. I'm not a drunkard, I just like drinking occasionally,' I replied with twisted lips.

'Anyways, ignoring what you say, it's the identity of our relationship. That's the place where we recognized our feelings; we got to know each other.

'Adie, you know, I intentionally took you to *Retro.* I believe, you can know someone's real self when one's drunk. That's the time your mind doesn't control you. You are driven by your true self, your subconscious.' I loved her expressions when she preached.

'I thought you liked me at first sight while you were performing on the stage,' I smirked.

'So true, but I loved you after spending that evening with you.'

'What was so special?'

'I had an impression that you were high headed, rigid and self-centered.'

'And, how did you get that?'

'Of course, from what I had heard about you from Charlie.'

'Did he tell you about all those qualities of mine?'

'Not really, I interpreted so.'

'Then, how did you change your opinion.'

'I saw your actual self. You are a person of your own mind, however, easy going and flexible. You can't be influenced easily, but it doesn't make you rigid and self-centered in anyways. You are soft and courteous with the opposite sex. It's impossible for you to hurt a girl.

'I loved every bit of you,' Presha said, pressing her face on my chest.

Embracing me, she raised her head, looking at my face. Her wine filled eyes were enough to elate me.

'Now it's your turn to confess!'

'What? Yeah, you are right, it was the night, I felt a feeling sinking in me that life was impossible sans you. I know, I'm a debonair and girls get crazy on my first look. But, I found you different—no doubt you were attracted towards me, but nothing beyond that. I didn't find lust anywhere in your behavior. I realized you liked my inner self and not the body I was wearing.'

'Oh! What else?'

'Initially, I thought you were only a flamboyant girl and that's why you took me to that bar, but after you were drunk, I found you to be an intelligent and smart girl. The way your eyes were exploring my each expression told me what you were up to.'

'Great! Say something else.'

'Most importantly, I knew beforehand what I was entering into— I found you an obstinate girl, convincing you could be like a seasoned swimmer drowning in a splash pool.'

After that there was a silence between us; I could see, Presha was not so pleased with my last judgment, but then, there was no point in lying to her.

In those beautiful and peaceful surroundings, I heard a sound of glass being smashed on the floor; it was Presha, her voice was cracking like glass pieces.'

'So this is your genuine opinion of me. I feel that I have befooled myself about our relationship all this year. I thought you loved me from the core of your heart. But, now, I know, you entered into a contract so you can test your skills of handling a stubborn person.

'Charlie was so right; whenever he spoke about you, he always said you like doing crazy things, and now I feel marrying me is one of them.

'No wonder! You couldn't take an off from work even on our first anniversary. Everyone considers this as an important event in their life but you, you wanted an off from the obstinate lady.'

I heard females could be as unpredictable as weather, but, the day I experienced it for the first time.

'Presha, you have always longed to hear the truth; otherwise, you can start micro-expression reading any time,' I said, sarcastically.

I paused and said, 'Moreover, I'm not saying anything unusual. I'm sure several people would have told you the same thing.'

I never expected my remark to be the last blob of chili sauce, which could have put Presha on fire.

'Enough! I'm not here to understand how recalcitrant you feel am I?

'Disgusting!

'Gauche! I'll be imprisoned with you for two days on this island.'

'Presha, you are nuts. I know you are crazy, but this is the extreme.

'I said something casual; it was a cool breeze, and you have turned it into a tornado.'

'Bullshit! Cooool breeze? Do you have any idea of sensitively handling a girl?'

'Bloody hypocrite! You love, honesty, but you can't hear the truth.

'And what nonsense are you saying? I can't handle a girl? Are you a girl?

'Grow up Presha, accept this new phase of life. I can't take your idiosyncrasies forever,' I said, losing complete control over myself.

'Shut up! Don't you dare to talk to me after this,' Presha yelled at me.

'Hell with you! I'll tolerate you for two days and then we need to rethink about our relationship,' I said. I had spent $20,000 on bookings. It was difficult for me to let them go down the drain so I showed no intention of returning back, before two days.

'Fine. I know, I'm a nice and compassionate person. I'll let you attend this conference. But, after that, for sure, I'm going to show you my extent of stubbornness.' Presha obliged me with her kindness.

We were quiet for some time, our faces turned in opposite directions. But our heart beats were loud and clear, echoing in the sea and striking our ear drums.

'Sir, you have reached the island,' a voice said piercing the echo.

'Thank you,' I said, getting off the boat. I offered my hand to Presha, and without wasting a second, she held it and disembarked the boat.

Our heart beats got to normal, a smile was visible on our faces. Perhaps, it was the magic of the place which had stunned us at the first sight.

A cute lady at the reception asked us about our choice of villa. I looked at Presha to see her facial expressions if she had been able to find out my surprise.

To my astonishment, I found Presha staring at the guy, seemingly German, standing next to the receptionist. I felt awkward. I had gone there to celebrate my first wedding anniversary and my wife was busy gazing other men. In the past too, on several occasions I had observed Presha behaving in a strange way, she gave lots of attention to men wherever she went. At times, I had even found her getting stuck to the waiters in a restaurant. Her behavior had been nagging my mind for quite some time, but, I preferred not to discuss it with her.

I patted her on the shoulder,'Presha choose a villa.'

'What do you mean? Haven't they told you at the time of booking,' Presha smiled.

'Ma'am, the whole island is booked for you,' Receptionist said.

'Now that's a surprise!' Presha was agog.

'I knew from the very start that you were lying to me, and it was no conference. But I was enjoying the effort you were putting in to surprise me.

'Adie, this is really amazing! I could have never dreamt of this extreme of yours.'

'To know my true extremes, you need to pay me attention,' I said, a bit sarcastically.

'Oh, Baby! I'm sorry for my offensive behavior.' Presha related my remark to the quarrel we had few minutes back, but I was referring to something else. Anyways, I allowed to let it go.

'I'm sorry too, for being so childish.'

But the reality was the flirtatious behavior of Presha, which she had been exhibiting every now and then, was bothering my mind. It was getting difficult for me to comprehend this change in her. I admired Presha for her dedication, candidly, my belief was shaking now.

I had spent an enormous amount of money in making the arrangements; it wasn't wise on my part, to allow anything to disturb our most important day not to be the most memorable day of our lives. With the spirit of unending love for Presha in my heart, I let every negative thought go away.

I looked at Presha; there was a radiance on her face. She was ecstatic. I found love for me beaming all across her. Maybe, arguments with her had disturbed my male ego; otherwise, she was her true self.

I embraced and kissed her. Taking her into my arms, 'Give us the best one of your choice,' I said to the girl at the reception.

She called a boy and said something to him, which was beyond our scope of understanding as she spoke their native language: Bahasa Indonesia.

'Please come along with me, Sir,' the boy said, pushing our luggage trolley.

Undoubtedly, it was a heaven. Sparkling water striking the white sand of the beaches looked like pearls spattering on the clouds wandering on the ground. It embossomed lush green trees, dancing to the tunes of the cool breeze. It was nature at its best.

Presha held my hand tightly. The warmth of her hand and serenity of the surroundings were enough to inebriate my soul. The sound of breath, of two of us, was disturbing the tranquility of the environment. I looked at Presha. She seemed to have attained nirvana. The day I realized, there was lots more turbulence inside Presha than that was visible to the outside world. Her thoughts were so deeply layered, in her mind and heart that it was difficult to comprehend her.

People like her are flying their life aircraft with two engines of heart and mind; they turn it off and on into a fighter and a passenger plane erratically, and no one knows which engine will be working when.

But, for my life, Presha was the plane I boarded to reach to its destination.

I filmed those moments in my eyes; and I usually screened them in my heart, whenever I felt lost. Presha looked beautiful; she appeared serene as if she had given unrest of her life to the sea; her eyes seemed like two magical glasses reflecting my image. I knew she loved me more than anything else in life.

'Sir, this is your paradise for the day,' the attendant said, escorting us into a perfectly crafted wooden structure with pastel colors all over on curtains, bed, and upholstery.

'Awesome! I couldn't have thought of anything more beautiful than this,' Presha remarked, hugging me. The environment was playing its tricks. Presha's emotions were soaring like high tides. She was getting impatient to be with me.

'Thanks. If we require anything we'll call you,' Presha said, handing over $50 to the boy as a tip. She was behaving like a self-proclaimed queen. Anyways, I succeeded in my mission of giving her a lifetime experience.

Next day, till twelve o'clock, we were swimming in the pool of passion. It was remarkable that not even once she mentioned about going to the pub. Eventually, I had superseded her obsession for bars. The excitement was spread in the air. It was rejuvenating.

'Happy Wedding Anniversary,' I wished Presha.

'Happy Anniversary to you too, and thanks for accepting me the way I am.

'Thanks for letting me the person I am; thanks for the patience you show when I challenge it every now and then with my eccentricity; and above all, thanks for the love you have showered on me always.'

'Wait! Wait! I can't take this much. I know the eternal truth is– I love you, and I can't live without you,' I said kissing Presha.

There was a lull for the moment. I was feeling blessed. We were made for each other.

'Let's go to our destination– where two souls meet,' said Presha.

Oh, no! I knew, anytime her destination could be a bar, and I had made arrangements for that too. We were there till dusk, till the time she was unconscious, and I carried her back to the room.

Next day, we woke up in the afternoon for another fun-filled day awaiting us. Passion, food, wine, dance and wildness were our friends; till, it was the time for us to check out.

As we moved out to embark on a boat, Presha shared a glance with the same German guy who was there at the reception on the first day. I was observing her closely. She smiled and blushed. Her lecherous behavior had started niggling me. She was turning out to be a natural flirt, her conduct was giving me tremendous stress, enough to take me to the grave.

'I hope you still wanna go back with me,' I said.

'What do you mean?' Presha pretended to be innocent.

'You know what I'm talking about. You seem to be awestruck by that guy,' I said without giving any efforts to hide my irritation.

'Rubbish. Who was he? Adie, you know I don't like such jokes,' Presha said, getting upset.

'I don't think it's a joke. You need to be true to yourself,' I said, still sticking to my stand.

'Adie, for heaven's sake, stop preaching to me about honesty.'

'Oh! Sorry, you are the mother of honesty; it completely slipped out of my mind! My apologies.'

'Nonsense. Don't spoil my mood,' Presha was furious.

'Do you really think if anything is left?'

'Go to hell! I give a damn to what you think.'

'No wonder,' I said, clenching my lips.

It wasn't surprising! We didn't look at each other till we reached back home. None were in a mood to compromise. Presha opened the door, kicked off her shoes and threw them in the air. She behaved like a typical brat when in anger. Next thing, I knew, she was going to open a bottle. She did exactly the same, a big drunkard she was.

Three days passed by and she didn't show any inclination to talk to me. I was feeling cramps in my stomach. Presha was capable of doing anything, but somewhere inside me I was sure she loved me, and she'll not take a drastic decision. But by that time I had realized, things had worsened and merely my belief in her love wasn't going to resolve any issue.

I was baffled; I wasn't able to find a way to approach her without offending my ego.

Dec 6, 2008: I was sitting alone on the terrace sipping my cup of bed tea and reading the newspaper. No, Presha wasn't on hunger strike; but as she had boycotted me, she was averse to anything prepared by me. Anyways, I was missing her.

It was the time I used to be interested in reading the newspaper; but I couldn't have dared to do it, as it was also the time for the live telecast from Presha. She would go on nonstop presenting her philosophies, views on the world events and solutions to most of the world problems. Several of her suggestions were quite unique and made lots of sense. I had often motivated her to write her advice to Mr. Bush and Mr. Singh, as the latter might find it useful for pertinent Indian issues and the former might be able to resolve most of the world problems. But Presha was a genius, she would reply to me that politicians weren't interested in any solutions; if they were, they knew it best as to what should be done, as they were the creators of most of the problems.

No wonder, even God has made a rose with thorns, nothing is perfect in this world. So there wasn't anything wrong if Presha had some quirks. I was feeling guilty for my behavior. I wanted to apologize. But believe me, this wasn't easy; if the man was as egoistic as Adie, and the woman was Presha– headstrong.

While I was flipping through the paper, suddenly my eyes widened and I grinned in amazement. It was like God appearing before my eyes, a miracle. It was an ad of *Singapore National University* for the next session. I remembered Presha having expressed her desire to pursue graduation. She might have left behind her dream, but I could still think of what might invigorate her.

I rushed to our bedroom where Presha was lying lifeless.

'Nightingale, look what I've found for you,' I said, putting my hand on her face. She brushed aside my hand and turned her face to the other side. I knew she was annoyed and I would have to take her tantrums as a blessing.

'Sweetie, I know I have offended you, but you also know my love for you is above everything. I can do anything to make you happy,' I said, trying to be as cheesy as possible. After marriage, you don't even realize when a gentleman like me too gets into the shoes of a typical husband. Anyways, it was all for our happiness.

'Sham, Sham,' Presha yelled without even looking at me. She took out a pack of cigarette and a lighter from the chest and moved towards the balcony.

She was tense. She wasn't internally as strong a person as she posed to be. Presha was sensitive; despite it, I had no clue what had happened to her that she wasn't respecting my sensitivities.

I followed her to the balcony. I stood there watching her. Presha's tresses were falling on her flawless face. From where I was looking at her, her face looked like a yellowish orange sky sparsely covered by black clouds and a platinum crescent moon jutting out of her nose. She was so beautiful.

She took out a cigarette from the packet and held it in between the fingers of the right hand to light it. I pounced on the opportunity, holding the lighter from her hand, did the honors of lighting the cigarette. Presha took a deep puff and released her stress. She held the cigarette high with her wrist bent back and stood blank staring in the air. I moved toward her and embraced her.

'Presha, I know you are annoyed with me and you have every right to be so.

'I'm ashamed of my behavior, and I can assure you this won't be repeated. Please forgive me this time. At least, hear me out once. This is what you wanted to do. I think it can thrill you. You have a great potential, go for it,' I said, and I really meant it. Meanwhile, Presha was continuously releasing her tension, and I wasn't sure whether she even gave a damn to what I said.

I heard Presha sobbing. She was deeply hurt.

'Oh dear, I'm sorry. Do you want me to cry with you?' I said, hugging Presha, my eyes were wet and voice was trembling. Her tears gave me the jitters, and I felt like a devil.

I kissed all over her face. I wanted her pain to permeate inside me. Presha was unmoved. We stood there numb for some time, and then I rushed to the kitchen to prepare coffee for her. I could see from the bay window of our living room that she was still fagging.

I made two mugs of coffee.

'Have it, you'll feel better,' I handed over the cup to Presha. She took it from my hand without bothering to look at me.

'I don't know what has gone wrong with you, Adie; but I'm warning you, this is your last chance. I'll not take this shit from you anymore.'

'I told you, I'm sorry,' I said, slipping my hand on her silky cheek.

'I'm keeping the newspaper on the table, give it a thought.

'It's difficult for me to leave you at this moment, but I have an urgent meeting lined up in the office.'

'Please go,' Presha said, brushing up her tears.

Within no time, I was ready to leave for my office.

Chapter 5

I was five minutes late for the meeting, which, of course, as anticipated, wasn't relished by anyone present there. Their arched brows and twisted lips irked me; aura in the room was pushing me to believe as if I had committed a crime by not being there on time. I was Adie, not born to take dictates from anyone. I was determined to give back the crap to them in the room itself. I condemned every suggestion put forth by my colleagues and presented my unique ideas on all the issues. In a fit to massage my super ego, I had been singled out. At the end of the meeting, I could see the astonishment on everyone's face; perhaps, it was due to my changed behavior. We moved out of the meeting room, and as usual, I got involved in my core job.

While going back home, I bought a bouquet of fresh red roses for Presha. I wanted to leave everything behind me and start afresh.

I presented the bouquet to Presha; It looked my gesture didn't exhilarate her, but she wasn't upset either. It was enough for me; at least, she had started normalizing.

When you expect the least, surprises, even in small packets can give you a larger than life happiness. Presha had prepared butter chicken for the dinner, and I was ecstatic at the thought. I wasn't sure whether it was the power of delicacy that made me delirious or the fact, Presha had cooked it for me.

I helped Presha in setting the table. Butter chicken wouldn't have been so scrumptious had it not been the red wine accompanying it. It was the best dinner I had in my life.

Presha, dressed in a blue jumpsuit with her black silky long hair covering her back, looked gorgeous. *A woman with no makeup, but the glow of sincerity and honesty written on her face has a high level of sex appeal.* This was more than often right for Presha.

'I have checked the admission details of *SNU* on the net. I'll go for it,' Presha declared in an authoritative tone.

'Fantastic! Let me know when I need to pay the fee.'

'No, thanks. I have already applied for a loan, and I'll take some part time job to meet my daily expenses.'

'It means you are still annoyed with me,' I murmured.

'Nothing like it. I always wanted to be independent.'

'Presha, you're free to do anything, and I'm not the kind of a person who'll ask you to do something against your wish.

'But if you still believe in me, enjoy your life and have fun in everything you do there. Rest, leave it to me. I'll take care of it.'

'Okay…,' Presha said after thinking for a minute. Maybe, my folded hands and knitted brows, earned me some sympathy.

'Can we now move on to our hanging paradise?' I said, smirking.

'Bastard!' Presha whispered with a smile.

Next morning, 'I'm not sure about you, but I had a fantastic night. I felt a hell lot of freshness in our relationship,' I gagged.

'It's even true for me,' Presha said with a lovely smile.

'Wonderful! Then let's have some planned wrangles in between. Lighting a match stick is enough to blow a fire in you,' I said. I think, it was a slip of the tongue, or I was overexcited.

'You better behave yourself. I'm not a waste bin who's there to collect any garbage from you,' Presha said roving her eyeballs.

'Okay, let's agree to embrace our bickering with both the hands if it occurs naturally. It adds spice to life.'

'Too much of the spice can cause ulcers,' Presha was as sharp as she can be in her tone.

I decided it was time for me to get ready for the office before I get entrapped into any further discussions with her. For the time being, I had exhausted all energy to cajole Presha.

'Listen, I'll be going out for shopping today. Do you want anything for yourself?'

'Nothing on the top of my mind. I'll call you if something strikes me. Anyways, we can again go for shopping this weekend.'

'You know, I like going alone.'

'Yeah, sure, I remember it,' I said, rushing out of the apartment as I was already late.

Life started moving smoothly. Presha got through *SNU* and her session was to begin on the first Monday of August.

6 Aug 2009: It was the freshmen inauguration ceremony at Presha's college. She was energized to make a new beginning. Presha was dressed up in a blue skirt and white polka dot top. She was looking graceful, very professional.

I wished her good luck with a light hug, and she left for the college. I watched her from the balcony as she moved out of the apartment building, to go towards the train station.

I was happy for Presha. But all of a sudden, God only knows, what happened to me– I felt sulky. My face was drenched in sweat, and palpitation fastened. I experienced a feeling of loss. I knew this was the end of my life; Presha is never going to come back to me.

I was sinking. I called up a doctor and took an emergency appointment. I described my state and asked for an ambulance. Within no time, an ambulance was there outside my apartment building.

I was feeling breathless; I was immediately put on oxygen. When I reached the hospital, the doctor examined me to find it as an anxiety attack. My blood pressure was high. At that age, I could have never thought of any problem with my blood pressure.

I was admitted to a nursing room. Hardly any medication was given to me. I was advised to relax, and if feasible, sleep for some time. I was kept under constant observation. After an hour or so, my condition stabilized and I was recommended a counseling session with a psychiatrist. For a second, it was hard to believe my ears. Adie, the most successful person in every walk of life, was asked to meet a psychiatrist! I was sure they had gone crazy. Anyways, I couldn't have left without completing the treatment.

I called my assistant to inform him about my half day absence.

The doctor happened to be a very sweet lady, Maria. She had tranquility spread on her face. I felt so relaxed with her, but I wasn't sure why I was sitting with her. Anyways, I could have spent hours listening to her.

She introduced herself and asked me about my background and other things in my life. It was nice chatting with her. I was opening up to her as if she was my childhood friend whom I had met after decades. I spoke to her at length about Presha. She was phlegmatically looking into my eyes. After some time, I was quiet, as I felt exhausted and there wasn't much left to be shared except about the petty bickerings between Presha and me. I think, that's the sign of normal, healthy married life. I didn't find any reason to tell her about it.

'Okay, you love your wife and she's equally fond of you. Right!' Practitioner stoically looked at me.

'Yes, we are made for each other.'

'What did you have for breakfast today?'

'Sandwich and coffee,' I said, frowning.

'Your wife is an excellent cook. Is it?'

'Ha ha ha...No, except she has learned to cook butter chicken well. We both are crazy about it.'

'Then, who prepares the meal at home.'

'Two of us; or whosoever has the time. Like, I prepared it today as it's her first day to the college.'

'College?'

'Yep, that's the time I felt sick when she was leaving and I looked at her from our balcony. I felt sulky as if I'm losing her forever.' I was finding everything ridiculous. Why was I telling all that to her? Such strange incidents do happen in life, but whether we need to ponder over them so much? And miss our critical work too 'cause of it.

'Doc, I need to rush to the office,' I said, without demeaning her efforts.

'Sure, Adie. I'll give you medicine, and recommend another session after a month.'

'Medicine? But I'm perfectly okay.'

'It seems, it's normal day to day stress; at times we don't feel it, but it's there in our subconscious mind,' Doc said coolly.

'Fine. Thank Doc,' I knew at the moment, I wasn't ever coming back to see her again.

Twelve o'clock: I reached office. I felt a sense of freshness to me as I greeted my colleagues. Perhaps, it was the charm of the lady that had given me a new energy. I smiled at myself, and before I could realize I was absorbed in my work.

I wanted to be back at home before Presha. I was sure she would have lots to share with me.

I dropped in at 5:30 p.m. Presha wasn't there. I was happy as I would get some time to prepare a few things for her. Those days, I kept experimenting with my newly acquired culinary skills. The day I planned to grill chicken kebabs, which I had marinated in the morning when Presha was getting ready for her college. Besides, I quickly chopped the vegetables for soup. While I was preparing some cheese sandwiches for Presha, there was a bell at the door.

"It must be Presha."

As I opened the door, she hugged me tightly.

'Oh, Adie! What a beautiful day!' Presha said with a gleam in her eyes.

'Let's go inside and I have my ears, anxiously, waiting to hear you,' I told her trying to sound as romantic as I could have. You can't stretch boundaries beyond your natural elastic limits.

'Campus is so beautiful, vast and greenery all around. I made friends with my new classmates.'

'No wonder! You are anyways superb at it,' I said innocently.

'What do you mean?' Presha was taken aback by my remark.

'I'm commending your knack for creating friends wherever you go.'

'I can take your words. I can see you are not lying.

'Adie, Guess what? Who's there in my batch?'

'At least, I'm not,' I said.

'Not Funny! Yuvi!'

'Yuvraj Singh, Indian cricketer!'

'Adie, you know what?'

'Tell me.'

'Your sense of humor is rotting day by day.

'Yuvi, was my classmate in middle school. His father had a transferable job so they left Kolkata when we were in the sixth standard. Baba could have asked me to marry him if the decision was left to him,' Presha was perked up.

'You are so elated as if God has given you a second chance,' I said coolly.

Candidly, I was feeling uncomfortable from inside. I couldn't assign the reason to my restlessness, but I wanted to be rude with Presha. Every other male excited her and she gave them too much attention. Before she came in, I was so cool, like a calm sea, suddenly there was a tsunami inside me. I could feel needle pricks on my body. My lips were pursed and fists tightly closed. I was trying to control myself from saying anything to Presha. She was insouciant about my concern on her flirtatious behavior.

Presha came out after freshening up. She bloomed like a flower, but to me, she looked like a cactus. The desire in me to pamper Presha had fizzled out. I lay down the table, though, I was feeling indifferent.

Presha was so excited to see the table. I knew, she was overwhelmed with the thought of studying again with her childhood friend. Whatever I did for her was just an excuse to express her hidden feelings– she was elated to meet Yuvi.

'Wow! What a treat!' said Presha.

'I thought, you'll be hungry after a long day,' I strained myself to speak.

'What has happened to you, Adie? You are subdued. You have done so much, it's a real luxury!' Presha's over excitement was killing me.

'I hope you like it.'

'Of course!

'How was your day?'

'Not so bad,' I didn't feel like sharing with her what I had gone through.

Presha continued with her recital of the day. I was quietly listening to her, not entirely focussed on what she was saying. When she stopped babbling, it was already nine o'clock. I wanted to give an end to the enigmatic day. The most successful, intelligent and dashing Adie had to visit a psychiatrist. This was worse than the worst nightmare. My identity was being challenged, but I was perplexed why it was happening to me.

I wasn't happy with Presha's behavior, but then she was an independent person and had every right to follow her way. Actually, the feeling of betrayal was acting like a slow poison gradually killing me.

I felt withdrawn from Presha, and without giving a damn to her feelings, soon, I was in slumber.

Late at night, I heard Presha talking to someone over the phone. I was sure it was Yuvi– newly discovered love of Presha.

When I opened the eyes in the morning, Presha lay beside me, staring at me. She ran her hands through my hair. Her caress prompted me to believe that she was my Presha, who once, only adored me. She was captivated by me.

"What has changed in me? Why is she shifting her interest?" I asked myself.

'What are you looking at?' I asked Presha.

'I'm counting your gray hair.

'Adie you are just thirty-one, but the pace at which, your hair are graying, very soon you'll look sixty,' Presha said, smugly smiling.

'Who were you talking to yesterday night after I slept?' I said, ignoring her remark on my hair.

'Charlie.'

'Why did you call him so late at night?'

'He called me to ask about my first day in the school.'

'Was it your first day at pre- school?'

'Adie, you have a fantastic sense of humor. But, dear, he's my brother and he has every right to call me whenever he feels like,' Presha said, without realizing my undertone.

'You should have spoken to him if you were awake. He missed you,' Presha said.

'How do I know whom you were talking to?'

'Then at night, I couldn't be talking to any stranger, and you know my family and friends,' Presha remarked calmly.

'But I don't know Yuvi.'

'Oh yes! I should invite him to dinner on this weekend,' Presha blushed.

'Yes you can, but I'm not there.'

'Why? Where are you going?'

'I have some work in the office.'

'Both days, you'll be in the office.'

'Yep.'

'Fine. We can have it next week.'

'That's better,' I took a sigh of relief as if I had postponed my torture for a few more days.

'Okay, I'll make a move. I don't want to be late for the first day of class,' Presha said, and walked to the kitchen.

We had bed tea together; we were quiet most of the time. Presha was entangled in her thoughts, and I was trying to guess what she was thinking. She finished her tea; scooting off the bed, she kissed me and proceeded for daily chores. I was confused, sometimes I felt she loved me more than ever and the next moment I was disturbed by her. Anyways, it was time for me to prepare for a hectic day ahead.

* * * * *

I reached the office on time. Everything was same there, but the moment I entered inside, I felt the aura had a different positive energy.

'Hey buddy,' I said to a guy sitting in the bay adjacent to the entrance door. He smiled and waved at me. As I was whisking through the corridor towards my chamber, I murmured, 'Good morning,' to everyone out there. But I could feel from their exceptionally broad smiles, there was something which I wasn't aware of. I reached my work area and plugged in my laptop. As soon as I logged in, a message popped up wishing me on being recognized as the *Employee of the Year*.

Now that was something amazing, not because I gave any credence to these awards, but I seriously needed some kind of recognition to boost up my morale. E-mails from friends and colleagues started flooding my mailbox, congratulating me on the achievement and exhorting a celebration.

Without discussing it with Presha, I decided to throw a bash on Saturday evening. It would have also saved me from the excuse I had given to Presha when she wanted to invite Yuvi at our place. I realized, recently I had started bluffing with Presha and she was unable to identify it, or perhaps, she intentionally ignored it.

I booked the private room of *Lime House* for the party and invited a select group of friends at 7:00 p.m. I liked the incredible jerk chicken served there, and moreover it gave us a choice to head off to a club there as the night progresses. I knew, Presha would be thrilled by the idea.

When I reached back, Presha wasn't home. Her pets greeted me with cheerful sounds. If she wasn't around, by default my first priority was to give attention to her pets, and by then mine too; though, they always considered Presha to be their own, and gave me a stepfatherly treatment.

I was eager to meet Presha. Hoping the clock will move faster, I started cleaning up the house which was usually left in an unkempt state in the morning. I picked up the towels from the bathroom floor; folded, the unused, but tried out clothes; and placed them back in the wardrobe. Cleaned the kitchen but didn't prepare anything for dinner as I had planned to take Presha out that night.

Presha was getting extremely late, it was nine o'clock and I didn't have a clue about her whereabouts. I tried to resist myself from calling her; thinking, she might consider it as an intrusion into her privacy.

Giving a damn to what she feels, I called her after some time.

'Where're you?'

'I'll be there in an hour or so. If it gets delayed, you go to sleep. Don't bother about my dinner. I already had it here,' Presha hung up the phone. She sounded a little irked.

I was furious at her response. I called her again.

'Hey, I asked where're you?'

'Adie, don't create a scene. I'm not a baby you need to be concerned about.

'How're you behaving?' said Presha.

'Damn it! I'm your husband and I have every right to know about you.'

'I had already sent you a message in the evening that I would be late. You should have checked your phone before calling me.

'Our class planned a dinner, and I'm out with them.'

'Who all is there?'

'Adie, now you are threatening my identity. Good night,' Presha banged the phone.

I immediately checked my phone to find Presha's missed message at four o'clock. But instead of sending an SMS, she could have called me. For an hour or so I was very upset. Presha wasn't still back.

I grilled a chicken sandwich for myself. I wanted to drink that day to release stress. I unintentionally followed Presha's footsteps to drink alcohol as a stress buster.

I fell on the bed; the noises of her pets were irritating me. I didn't know when my eyes were shut.

I woke up in the morning to find Presha still not there in the bed. I started brooding, and the idea of motivating Presha to join school seemed a howler. Suddenly, there was a sound of a door opening up, Presha came out of the washroom.

'Hey, Adie! Can you prepare some black coffee for me?'

'What happened? Did you drink yesterday night?'

'I puked for the last two hours when you were in coma. It seems you were also drunk; Amazing! You took whiskey last night.'

'How do you know?'

'Bottle on the table is displaying it.'

'How did you come back?'

'Yuvi dropped me.'

'He dropped you to this bed!' I was stunned at her.

'Hope so. I was unconscious, I don't know when…,' Presha remarked casually.

'Presha, how can you be so brazen? You are so coolly telling me, a stranger, and that too, a male, dropped you to our bedroom in an inebriated state!'

'Adie you are going crazy. I told you he's my childhood friend, and I have been always drinking with my buddies. I think you have forgotten our first meeting.'

'It was different. You are married now.'

'Nothing is different, except you are sick now. You are trying to act like a husband.'

'I'm not acting, but I'm your husband. You should maintain some decorum.'

'Hell with you!' Presha moved off from the bed to prepare coffee.

Like any other day, after a tiff, that day also we didn't bother to look at each other. We followed our ways.

Chapter 6

'Adie, you didn't tell me about the party on Saturday,' Presha said, as soon as she entered the house that evening.

'Did you give me a chance? You were not there the whole night.'

'Don't start it all over again.

'I met John on the tram, and he asked me if I was all set for the party. It was too embarrassing to pretend in front of him. What's it all about?'

'I have been selected as *Employee of the year*; and on friend's insistence, I have arranged a small get together at the place of your choice.'

'Oh Adie, I know no one can love me like you. You are the best,' Presha said, hugging me.

'But now you don't love me. You only like your independence.'

'Yep, I love my identity since my existence is due to what I am, but you are an indispensable part of my identity. I can't exist without you.'

Any reassurance from her, about her love for me, would assuage distrust for her. I felt happy.

'You told me you had some work in the office this weekend,' Presha reminded me with all good intentions. She was never the kind who would be indirect or sarcastic.

'I'll manage,' I said, avoiding eye contact with Presha.

'Then I'm inviting Yuvi and Mike as well.'

'Now, who's this Mike?' I said.

'He's a friend. He's in my class.'

'Presha, for you everyone is a friend; but this is a private party, only close friends are invited.'

'Yuvi and Mike are close friends.

'Let me think, what I'm going to wear that day,' Presha said without bothering about my concern.

I didn't like her affinity for her friends, but she was hardly paying any heed to my feelings. I knew Presha was very soft hearted and a little flirtatious too; she could have easily fallen into the trap of pseudo-friendship. She wasn't ready to listen to my viewpoint.

* * * * *

5th Sep 2009, Saturday 6:30 p.m.: Presha and I were at the restaurant, a little before the scheduled time. Presha decided to wear the gown, which she had bought for our wedding, but didn't wear due to her Ma's objection. As usual, she looked beautiful. Her glowing tanned skin, deep-set black twinkling eyes, pouty lips, raven hair and angular figure made her look distinct. The only thing missing was an innocent smile. Presha always had a serious face. I wish if she could have taken a little bit of my advice and smiled, a smile would never let anyone's brain drain out.

Soon, my friends arrived. It was a party to celebrate my success, but rather, it was turning out to be a forum to celebrate Presha's new life–college life. My friends were more interested in congratulating her and listening to her anecdotes about the college. It had for all time proven out to be a Presha's show.

A few people were gracious enough to involve themselves in a conversation with me when they saw me standing alone in a corner. It was not a feeling of being left out, but definitely, I found Presha to be the cynosure of all eyes.

And finally, Presha simpered. Piercing through the crowd arrived two young men; seeing them, she rushed towards the guys. I hadn't met any of them, yet I could make out, they were Yuvi and Mike. Yuvi was attached to her roots, but Mike looked like a local guy.

Presha was thrilled to see them. She hugged them tightly. Yuvi wasn't so comfortable with her gesture and withdrew himself as soon as possible. Mike was exhilarated, he kissed Presha on her cheeks and embraced her; he glanced at her eyes for a few seconds before leaving her.

It was embarrassing for me. I was ruffled.

Presha briskly moved towards me, holding Mike's hand.

'Adie, meet my friends Mike and Yuvi. Two are amazing guys.'

'Yuvi, you have already told me should have been in my place. Mike, just now I have seen doing wonders for you.'

Presha smiled wryly and said, 'Okay guys! Let's forget ourselves for some time. Please move to the bar.'

'You have already let everything slip from your mind, like, you are a married woman and not a high school girl anymore. We all should go to the bar, but, you, be here.'

'You are testing my patience, Adie,' Presha murmured.

'Who cares?' I replied back with equal acrimony.

Yuvi came forward and patted on my back. He invited everyone to the bar. I was furious. My heart was beating fast. I felt like breaking something or hitting someone. Controlling my hatred for Presha and her friends was difficult. I tried my best to restrain myself.

After a while, when everyone was almost sinking in the wine, a female colleague of mine accidentally stepped on Mike's foot. She lost her balance, and a glass in her hand splashed on Mike's shirt. There was something exceptional in him; he was making females intentionally or unintentionally, fall on and fall for him.

Mike was smartly dressed in a pair of blue denim jeans, and a white see through shirt.

He smiled at my colleague, and very freely took off his shirt in the presence of everyone. The sound of *Wow* echoed the place as all eyes fell on his six pack abs. I immediately looked at Presha's face and her adoring eyes. All of a sudden, I reached out to him and slapped him. He was stunned, rather everyone present there was frozen. Nobody could realize what went wrong. There was anger in Mike's eyes and before he could react, Presha approached me.

'What nonsense, Adie? What has happened to you?' Presha yelled at me.

'This bastard doesn't know how to behave in public. Look at him; he took out his shirt in front of everyone.'

'Are you crazy? What else could have he done? It's all wet.'

'I can understand Presha, you can go to any extent to justify him.'

'Ridiculous!'

Presha turned her face towards Mike and said, 'I apologize on behalf of Adie. I'm disgusted by his behavior. Thank you for staying calm. I appreciate the favor you have extended by not reacting.'

'I'll kill him. I know how you must be planning to return his favors,' I said, moving aggressively towards Mike. My friends held me back. Presha apologized to everyone and that's how our evening ended. She didn't even wait for me and left the place.

It was good that she had left alone. I was so angry with her, the way she had humiliated me in front of that rot, Mike, I could have thrashed her right there.

I avoided going back home and confronting Presha. I had a premonition; something fatal was going to happen that day. I was sitting in the bar cursing Presha for being a slut. It was time for the bar to close, and I was politely asked to leave the bar. I came out and moved towards the station. I took a train to *Palawan beach*. It was a calm place where I always felt relaxed.

I was sitting there for three hours. Sitting there, I was talking to myself for most of the time, but in between I cried over Presha's behavior. Other time flashes of her infidelity made me distressed.

I felt like talking to Muma. She was so right in her thinking about Presha. Presha wasn't a marriage material; she wanted to enjoy her life with everyone she met. If nothing else I wanted to kill myself. It was very late at night, so I avoided the idea of calling my mother. But I desperately needed to talk to someone. Charlie, though, was Presha's brother, yet had pleaded me not to marry her. He knew his sister so well. I was overwhelmed with emotions, I pressed Charlie's number.

'Hey, Adie! Is everything well? You are calling so late.'

'Sorry, I disturbed you,' I sobbed.

'What has happened, Adie? Are you crying? Where's Presha? Give her the phone.'

'She must be at home.'

'What do you mean by must be? You don't know?'

I burst into tears, and started to prattle, 'She was…now I don't know…she fought…I'm on a beach……'

'But, why are you crying? Is Presha ok?' said Charlie.

'Nothing has happened to Presha. She has made my life hell,' I screeched.

'Okay, calm down, and tell me the whole issue,' Charlie sounded anxious.

I told him everything; how she was cheating on me. She was a loose character.

'You stop bullshitting. I know her, she can be anything in this world, but never a bad character,' said Charlie.

'She's your sister, that's why you are shielding her now. Remember, a year back you told me not to marry her.'

'Adie, but that was because of her stubborn attitude, and free spirit.

'I never wanted two of you to marry 'cause of your similar nature; otherwise, she's a superb girl.'

'Charlie, I feel I have made a mistake by calling you up. You are too biased,' and I hung up.

I sat there; white sand glittering in the moonlight looked as if I was on the moon, which has come down to the earth. Indeed so, Adie, who used to be in the sky always, was lying shattered on the ground, crying on the infidelity of a female he loved the most. My life was slipping out of my hands. I knew I needed to control it before it got too late.

Rising from the ground, I sand off my clothes. Looking at the open silver sky, I squawked,

'Presha you are mine; you'll always be mine.' All my anger for Presha was gone, and I wanted to reach for my crazy girl as soon as possible.

I was home in around half an hour. I opened the door, *cluck…*, breaking the silence of the surroundings.

As soon as I entered the house, I heard Presha speaking to someone. I hastily took off the shoes at the door. It was dark, my hand struck the vase on the shoe rack and it thumped on the floor. With trembling hands, I switched on the light. I saw Presha standing on the balcony talking to someone over the phone. A part of me was relieved, and the other half was perturbed. Good, there wasn't anyone in the room, but who was over the phone at 4:00 a.m., was still to be unfolded.

She quickly disconnected the phone on seeing me. I took my eyes off her, and without uttering a word moved to the bed. I was drained out. For some time, I wanted to close my eyes from the world.

My eyes were shut, but still wide open. After a few minutes, Presha too came to the bed. We were lying there unaware of each other. At least, I was aware of where she had kept her mobile. I wanted to directly reach to her mobile to check the phone log; but I knew if Presha wasn't asleep, she would be on fire if she caught me. I waited patiently for some time. When Presha was still, and her breathing was rhythmic, I knew she had drowsed. I was scared as she was an anxious person, and I had never found her sound asleep.

Holding my breath, I slowly got off the bed; trying to fully balance my body so as to avoid creating any noise. She had kept her mobile on the side table. I picked up the mobile and sneaked out to the terrace. I sat on the floor hiding myself behind the chair and started cracking her password. I tried all the combinations of our names, relevant dates but didn't succeed in any one of them. It was the turn of her newly formed relationships, and I was horrified to decode her password as *Yuvi02122007*. Yuvi, and our wedding date. It was humiliating.

I went on to check her call log. The last call she made was with Mike at around twelve o'clock. She had called him five times after flouncing from Lime House. I further checked her calls, and the last call was received from Charlie at 3:40 a.m. Again, one-half of mine was pacified but the other was restless. I was sure Presha was getting closer to Yuvi and Mike; they were as much a part of her life as I was. I was assuming I was still there, but God only knew if I existed anywhere or not.

I was numb. Suddenly there was a rush of blood in me, and I moved inside.

Presha was lying on the bed unaware of the turmoil she had created in my life. She looked so calm and serene. I went near her; moving her hair at the back, I started licking her earlobes. I could realize Presha had woken up, but she was mesmerized by the sensation.

'Adie, you are hurting me,' Presha cooed.

I wasn't bothered about what she said or felt, I couldn't stop.

Suddenly, she shrieked and pushed me back with all might to throw me down on the floor. I got back to my senses and smelt something sour, foul. I felt short of breath and my mouth was dry as wood. I rolled my tongue on the lips and I tasted blood. I got panicked and flicked on the light switch. Presha lay there unconscious in the pool of blood. Blood was profusely oozing out of her earlobe. I had bitten it into two pieces.

I could have been behind the bars if I took her to the hospital. I was reluctant to take a chance, but on the other end, Presha's state was bearing hard on me, to do whatever it takes, to relieve her pain. I was afflicted by the guilt, and in a fit, I grabbed a metal toothpick to dig my lip. I wounded my lip in penitence.

I sat beside Presha, 'Presha open your eyes.

'I'm sorry.

'It was a mistake.

'It'll never happen again.

'Look! I have also been punished.'

It was in vain. She was unmoved. I realized that something needs to be done immediately. Blood wasn't stopping to flow. To top it all, my lip too was bleeding extensively. I thought of calling a doctor friend of mine, who was an Indian, for help. I rang him; fortunately, he picked up the phone. I told him that an accident had happened as I was drunk. I pleaded him for help. He knew me well, so he was supportive enough to extend his support by attending our case of emergency.

I called a cab for *Holland Village*, where my friend resided.

I picked up Presha, stained in blood, to put her in the cab. It reminisced about the day when I first carried her in my arms when she was insentient as she was drunk. Her spirits were high, confidence glowed on her face. But that day, it was pain and torture written all over her. I decided, to talk to her about everything disturbing me, I was anxiously awaiting for Presha to open her eyes.

Cab driver frowned on seeing us. It would have been a pathetic sight for anyone out there. He helped to put Presha in the car on my lap. I held her tightly in my arms. In between, I wiped her ear with cotton balls. When I dabbed cotton on her, it brought goose bumps on my skin. I could feel the pain she must be experiencing, but was not in a state to express it.

We reached the Holland Village, and, in fact, my friend was standing out on the road waiting for us. I felt he had gauged the seriousness of the situation over the phone as I had never sounded that distraught any time before.

He pushed us inside his house in a small room, which he used as his clinic. Luckily my friend was a renowned surgeon, so he could aptly handle it at home. He asked his wife to handle my case. Two of us were cleaned up and given a tetanus toxoid injection. Doctor compressed Presha's ear with a bandage to stop the blood. I was given cold compression on my lips.

Presha was administered a local anesthesia. Her earlobes were stitched together with sutures that needed to remain in place for one or two weeks. I was horrified thinking Presha's reaction about her condition. I wasn't sure even if she would stay with me or not, after knowing what I did to her. I was also afraid of the fact that she would move around with sutures as in no way, she would have missed her college for a long span. I was hounded by the twin fears of losing her forever, and legal risks, if she decided to open her mouth.

I hated myself for a moment. I was disgusted by my selfishness. I questioned my love for Presha; was it so short-lived that I was thinking of something else, apart from Presha's pain. I decided I would request Presha to brutally penalize me for my actions, and hand me over to the police for the abuse.

I was standing there by Presha's side, staring at her.

There was a pat on my shoulder. It was my friend. 'Adie, this is wild. I'll not ask you, how did it happen, but it might cost you your life,' said my friend.

'I know. But nothing was intentional. I was drunk and we flowed in love,' I said, hiding my embarrassment.

'Anyways, Presha needs to come back after a week to get the sutures removed.'

'Sure, we'll be there. I don't know how to express my gratitude. I'm indebted.'

'Don't bother. You take good care of her.'

I was sure I had failed to sham anything. He knew it wasn't love. I felt ashamed.

We came back home. Presha got into her consciousness, but she wasn't saying anything. She even avoided looking at me. I started crying and apologized, but she didn't move; she was stupefied.

I took her mobile and dialed Yuvi's number to inform him about Presha's absence from the school due to her ill health. He politely asked me about Presha's state and avoided any further talk. It might be due to my friendly behavior with Mike the previous day.

I knew Presha was wrong, but why was I getting monstrous. My intention was to get Presha back on track, and on the way, I had lost all the tracks. I told myself to be patient and in control of self. I promised if she forgave me for the last time, I'll never give her a chance to complain again.

I prepared coffee for her. Raising Presha's back and propping her up with pillows, I drew the coffee mug near to her lips, and she sipped! Honestly, I wasn't expecting a positive response from her. Again, ***true happiness comes in small packets when you least expect it***. Presha wasn't looking at me, but I dared to look at her to find out what's going on in her mind. She sipped half a mug, and then slightly raised her hand to tell me that she was done.

She tried to get down. I immediately got up from the bed and offered my both hands for the support. She ignored me. She held side rails of the bed to get down, and with wearied steps walked towards wooden chest in the room to take out a cigarette and lighter.

She went to the terrace. I saw her puffing, like anyone's guess—either she was stressed out by the anger for me, or by the love of Mike. She was in deep thoughts. I didn't find it proper to disturb her by my presence there, so I moved to the kitchen to prepare some clear vegetable soup and cheese sandwiches for breakfast.

I was in the kitchen dishing up the morning meal for her, and as I turned back, to take the toast out of the grill, I found Presha standing there. She was staring at me, and seeing her there I fumbled for words.

'What was that?' Presha was phlegmatic.

'I'm sorry.

'I have no words to condemn my horrendous act.

'I can only apologize.

'Presha, if possible, please forgive me.

'I love you, and this is the only truth,' I said with wet eyes.

'Mr. Aadir, I had always wondered if love can turn someone into a sexual beast, and last night, I think you manifested it.

'Moreover, you were drunk, and as per my old belief, you are your actual self in such a situation.

'So, almost after two years of marriage, I realize you are a sexual beast,' Presha smirked.

I never understood that woman. What went inside her, was impossible to gauge. She took the brutality in stride, and wrapped up the matter by just calling me a *sexual beast*.

'By the way, I didn't like your behavior with Mike yesterday. I was abashed, broken from inside,' said Presha.

'I didn't like the way he was getting closer to you, and tried impressing you.'

'He's close to me; that's why he's a friend. Who gave you the right to beat someone, who's closer to me?'

'Love,' I said emphatically.

'No, it's an ugly shade of love– over possessiveness.'

'Presha, I don't care whatever it is, but I don't want you to make friend with Mike and Yuvi.

'You don't know how wicked men are.'

'Adie, I'm matured enough to handle myself.'

'You think so, but the reality is you are still a small girl living in some dreamland.'

'I don't know, but I find you a cute typical Indian male who is overtly possessive about his wife. And he considers her to be his possession.'

'Nonsense! It's so untrue. I'm a male, and I can observe a few things about this gender, better than you,' I said. I avoided telling her that I can see a few things about her as well, which are shameful.

'Two of them are great guys and I don't find any problem with them.

'No promises, but I'll try to be cautious with them.'

'It'll be a great favor.

'Can you have breakfast now? It's ready,' I said.

We finished eating, Presha was feeling drowsy, she went off to sleep.

The day I had taken an off from the office. While Presha slept, I got involved on my laptop doing some work from home.

The phone buzzed, it was from Charlie. He was standing outside the building entrance. I entered the code, and within no time, there was a bell at our door.

'Hey, buddy! What a deadly surprise!' I said, hugging Charlie.

'Hey, are you guys okay?'Charlie asked in a muted tone.

'What can happen to us, dear Charlie?'

'No, it's just that Presha knows I'm coming. Didn't she tell you?' Charlie said, standing in the doorway.

I was offended by Charlie's remark so I needed to give it back, 'When you know we had a quarrel yesterday, I think you shouldn't point out a finger at our relationship.

'You can choose to blame me for whatever you want, but please, do come in,' I said smiling.

'Let me see Presha first, then I'll decide the culprit,' Charlie said, ignoring the acrimony in my voice. His eyes anxiously looked for Presha.

Presha woke up by the noise two of us created. She raised her back with the support of her hands, almost sitting there, she said,'Welcome Dada!'

It was for the first time I heard her calling Charlie as *Dada*. I felt a strengthened bond between them. So, the man in front of me was Presha's brother, and no longer my best friend. It was a change, though, not much to my liking.

'So, Charlie you are here to see how happy our life is,' I said. I still had not been able to digest his sudden arrival.

'It's been a while we met. I just wanted to have fun with you guys,' Charlie said acting like a matured big brother, which I thought he always was.

'Welcome to this mini zoo of Presha and Adie!,' finally I accepted him in our home, though, I was sure he knew something was wrong with two of us, and he was there to sort it out.

'What has happened to your lips?' Charlie asked looking worried.

I looked at Presha, and her ears were covered with hair, it seemed, which she had done intentionally to hide her wound.

'Courtesy Presha's ear studs,' I said wickedly. Charlie was embarrassed beyond limits and immediately took off his eyes from my lips.

'Presha why are you looking so exhausted?' Charlie said.

'You know Dada I was up till 4 a.m. talking to you, and then this incident with Adie happened, so I didn't sleep properly.'

'Charlie, check out my culinary skills. They have improved drastically,' I said, serving sandwiches and soup, which I had prepared for the breakfast.

'I was actually starving.

'Nice. Indeed!' said Charlie.

'It's no butter chicken, but you are a man of few needs, Charlie; you have the knack to please others,' I said, patting Charlie's back.

'Okay guys, there's some news; I'm here for a purpose.

'There's a marriage proposal for me, the girl is here in Singapore. She's working with a bank.

'Presha, you know her; she's Yuvi's cousin, Priyanka,' said Charlie with a broad smile.

'Oh, Dada! She's an epitome of beauty!'

'Brain too. She has done her MBA from Wharton Business School,' Charlie was proud to talk about her.

'Why in this world she'll marry you?' I remarked.

'What's wrong with me? I'm qualified. I agree, not that good looking, but no doubt a pleasing personality.

'Above all, she's a *Bong* from our community and our parents are very much interested in this alliance.'

'Charlie, don't you feel you are falling short of positives except, except, you are a *Bong;* she's from your community and your parents are keen on it,' I said in a casual manner, though, with full intentions of teasing Charlie.

'Dada has always been an obedient son unlike me— a typical brat.

'There's no harm in pleasing your parents. At times they do wonders for you,' said Presha.

'Look who's saying that. You have never cared about your parents, but now I think you are repenting,' I was sardonic, which had become a norm by then.

'Of course, you mature as you grow old. But that doesn't mean you repent; you just get a different perspective of looking at the things.'

'Like you think differently about Yuvi now,' it was getting impossible for me to manage my tongue.

'Yuvi! What about Yuvi?' asked Charlie.

'Dada, forget it. It seems Adie is fascinated by Yuvi. Every now and then, he wants to talk about him,' Presha said, trying to defuse the stress I had created in the environment.

Charlie was not a kid, he never was. He pretended to take the matter casually, but I knew he would have caught few strings which were enough for him to weave a rug.

'I don't know what you people are talking about; it's your personal matter. Let me go now for my date,' and Charlie left our place.

I could see from Presha's face, she was irritated by my remark on Yuvi. Presha had changed, no more she adored honesty.

* * * * *

Charlie came back at night, exhilarated about his day. After all, he got a chance to spend the day with a girl. He was more than gung-ho about the prospect of getting married to Priyanka. His alliance was a done deal. Next day, early morning he flew back to India.

Presha also joined her college back after a day's break, and I didn't have any choice but, but to go back to the office. I was embarrassed by the scene created in the party on Saturday. Internally, I was blaming Presha for inviting Mike there. He was vulgar.

A few inquisitive eyes rose as I entered the office. After some time, I was normal, busy in office schedule.

I had started living a piecemeal life; what next moment had in stored for me was never clear. I took a moment off, closed the eyes and stretched myself in the chair; a deep breath refreshed my body and mind.

The beep on the intercom broke into my tranquility. A colleague and a good friend of mine called me for the lunch in the cafeteria. I agreed to join him, as I wanted to speak with someone about Saturday's incident. He was the best guy for the purpose as he was present at the party, he knew me well and we synchronized in our thinking too.

I reached the cafeteria, and he was standing there waiting for me.

'Hey Adie, what's up?' he said.

'Morning was a bit lethargic. Still, the party's incident is howling my mind.'

'Forget it,' said my friend, trying to avoid any further discussions on the subject.

When we were seated I again tried broaching the topic of the party, 'I genuinely feel sorry for the incident. I apologize for the inconvenience caused to you guys.'

'It's okay, Adie. Such incidents keep happening in such gatherings.'

'No, it was repugnant. I wanted to kill that bastard, Mike, for the scene he created.'

'Adie, if you don't mind, you created the scene and not your guest. It was an accident and what he did was impulsive.'

'Impulse can only tell you what kind of a person someone is, he's indecent.'

'I think, you took it quite seriously, which was not required. It was a party mood.'

'No, the swine, was trying to catch my wife's attention. He's filthy,' I said with a raised voice.

'Cool down! Why are you getting so excited? We are merely talking about a situation,' he said.

'Do you think I'm mad?' I lost my temper.

'Adie the way you are behaving reflects so,' my friend was irritated.

His remark knocked down my all patience levels, and I picked up a glass of water placed on the table, and splashed it on his face.

'I don't care whatever you think now,' I moved out in a fit of rage.

In an attempt to justify my act that day I had deteriorated my image forever. I was the talking and laughing stock of the people, till the time I was in the organization. People avoided talking to me, even my good friends were cautious in discussing anything with me. I was labeled as grouchy. Just two bad incidents topsy-turvy my image. Adie, who was so popular among people for his great persona, was shunned away by this selfish world.

The day I reached home at nine o'clock, exhausted and disturbed. Presha was already there, preparing the dinner. It seemed two of us had resolved not to talk about last week's happenings. We took our dinner amicably; though, I was ruffled internally, yet I pretended to be composed.

Presha could read my mind, and poked me every now and then to know the cause of anxiety. It's not that I had anything against her, but I wasn't keen to share with her; rather, not with anyone in the world, not even with Charlie.

Presha was busy in her school, with assignments and friends. I had told her on several occasions that I didn't like her getting over-friendly with anyone, especially, with Mike and Yuvi. It was a weakness in her personality which she needed to work on. She rebuffed my thoughts; and alleged me of insecurity and over- possessiveness. But on the second instance, she told me that she liked my behavior as it thrilled her, the feeling of belonging was what she loved.

It looked to me as if she was keeping her hands with everyone, and she wanted to enjoy the best of both the worlds. Everyday bickering became the norm of our relationship. Presha was happy in her own world, and I was no longer attracted towards her. Presha's indifference to my concern bothered me; and acted as a venom, gradually taking me to the death bed.

Chapter 7

One of those days, I was asked about my willingness to travel to India for a three-month assignment. I promptly accepted, it would have given me a much-needed break from the role of a husband, and it had been a while since I met my parents. I was to travel a day after; it was for project evaluation of an existing client for their new project. It was strictly time bound.

I went back home and shared the news with Presha. She was apathetic initially. I thought the idea of staying away from me would depress her; rather, after some time she was excited, and she motivated me to take up the assignment with complete enthusiasm. She treated me like a kid by counting down the advantages of going to India. Nutshell, she wanted me to go as soon as possible. I could assign the reasons for her exuberance.

11th Sep 2009: I took an early morning flight to New Delhi, and by 6:30 a.m. I was at home with my parents and my sister. Rachel, my younger sister, had recently completed her Master's in management and was back home. She got a job in Delhi, giving her an opportunity to stay with parents for some time.

Rachel was a beautiful, intelligent and energetic girl. My sister was very much like me, a free bird. But I had always objected to the misuse of freedom by her. Guys had been humming around her for reasons anyone could have guessed. Instead of shunning them she had been encouraging them by flaunting her beauty. The way she spruced up was cheap and seductive.

Being an elder brother, I had loathed the stares of the guys at her; and on umpteen occasions, her boyfriends had been smacked by me. I was a cool headed guy, but when it came to Rachel, I burnt like a fire to protect her. She had consistently blamed me for holding a false opinion about her, and ruining her life with a patronizing attitude.

I wanted to save her from the trouble she could get into because of her over friendly nature and affinity for the opposite sex. Some or the other boy was at our home on the pretext of exchanging class notes with her. I had several times asked her if she had any girlfriends in her school; I had never seen them visiting our place. She had invariably rebuffed me on any such discussions and avoided answering me.

I was sure Rachel would bring a bad name to our family one day; I had told this to her on several occasions, and also to my parents several times. I had always been a great fan of Muma for her worldly wisdom. She knew there were always some issues among growing siblings, and eventually, they got settled down with time. She considered my over-protective attitude as one of those contentious issues. She believed in Rachel more than anything else in her life, and she equally adored two of us. Whenever I condemned Rachel's lifestyle, Muma reminded me of Rachel being an independent individual, who had every right to live her life, her own way– the way I wanted to live mine.

It's not that I didn't love my sister; she was the star of my eyes, but the difference in our ideologies had kept me away to express it to her.

In our otherwise peaceful home, a squabble between Rachel and me was the only cause of stress. After I had moved out of home for higher studies, things were better off. Rachel, anyways, was the darling of my parents so she was exhilarated to stay alone with them.

She also moved away from home after high school, for pursuing a degree in economics, and then management. So, after that we hardly got a chance to stay together for more than a week.

After eight years, we were to stay together for three months under one roof. I was excited to be with her after a long time. Our lives had enormously changed in those years. I hoped she had got a better exposure of the world by battling the odds alone, all those years. Even I got married and had a different perspective towards females. They are all same; no matter what, they can't stop from being coquettish. Rachel was no different.

Rachel couldn't attend our marriage as it was arranged in haste, and she had an exam on that day. Presha and Rachel had never met each other, but they were connected through Facebook. They spent lots of time chatting over the phone. They liked each other and were always in sync, except in their boundaries of freedom. Presha never had any limits, but Rachel due to our upbringing still believed in family values, and never, at least, experimented with alcohol.

While I was entering the house, Rachel came out running and hugged me. She was thrilled to see me, and so was I.

'Bro, where's Presha?'

'She had college to attend.'

'Oh! I need to meet her.'

'You can anytime fly down to Singapore.'

'I wish I can. I have recently joined a job, can't come for next six months, at least.'

'Forget it. Anyways, there's a high chance you'll be disappointed,' my remark wasn't intentional, but it just poured out, maybe, it reflected my inner self.

'Stop it, bro! I know how much you love her. Muma has told me everything about you two,' said Rachel.

I hugged Papa and Muma. Muma looked at my face with arched brows. My views about Presha might not have caught anyone's attention, but my mother's expressions told me that my remarks had raised several questions in her mind. She preferred to ignore them for the time being.

I felt sleepy, so I preferred to move into my room. I was refreshed to find it the way I had left it. My books, DVDs, music system, bean bag everything else was as is. Even wine bottles and the glasses hadn't changed their position. The only difference was about the photograph in the frame on the side table by the bed. The earlier picture had snobbish Adie, but the latest one had charming Adie and gorgeous Presha. It was our wedding photograph.

Presha was back in mind, and I was lost in her thoughts. I didn't realize when my eyes were shut. A knock at the door woke me up. It was Muma, calling me for lunch. I looked at my watch; it was two o'clock. Making myself comfortable in a pair of shorts and a T, I moved to the dining hall. Rachel was also sitting there in shorts and spaghetti. Her dressing sense irked me, and I couldn't control my anger.

'Rachel, you are a grown up girl and still you haven't gained decency in your dressing style.

'What you are wearing is disgusting. I thought time would have made you a sensible lot.'

'Adie you should better focus on your life, and leave me alone. I thought marriage would have changed something in you.

'But you are the same stupid person,' Rachel said in a sharp voice.

'You are sitting half naked in front of your father and brother.

'Is it our culture or has Muma taught you this?'

'Just shut up, Adie. Don't drag Muma in between.'

'Two of you stop fighting. The girl is of marriageable age and the boy is married, still you are at odds like kids.

'Adie, she's a grown up girl, she knows how to carry herself. It's not apt on your part to comment on her clothes.

'Your papa, and I'm okay with her lifestyle,' Muma said in a stern tone.

'What the hell I have to do if you guys aren't bothered. I'm telling you she'll create trouble for you one day,' I got up from the dining table and rushed back to my room.

I couldn't think of anything else except calling Presha to relax my mind. The phone was ringing, but Presha didn't pick it up. I called her again and again, Presha wasn't there. I had called her almost fifteen times. I was all the more restless.

Presha called back after five minutes, showing concern on the urgency I was in. I wanted to know where she was, that she couldn't attend my phone for so long. She told me she had gone to see off her friends who visited their home, and in a hurry, she had left the mobile in the apartment. I knew without saying that Yuvi and Mike were with her. Presha was becoming unmanageable. It was hardly any time since I left, and she was already partying with her salacious friends. I was put off by the thought so I banged the phone. Presha didn't bother to call me after that.

Next morning, I was in my new office. I was eager to experience the change, away from the turbulence going on in my life. Stunning! It was a small world. While I was entering the office, I couldn't believe, it was Akanksha following me. I was excited to see her. She had always been a quiet girl. We shook hands and got involved in a small tete-a-tete. She was a Director in the projects department, which meant I was to work with her for the next three months. I was delighted at the thought of working with a brilliant lady whom I had always admired.

She accompanied me to the CEO's chamber and introduced me to the elderly gentleman. After usual handshakes and the intro, we discussed the project. I was glad to be on the ground with the right minded people.

I spent rest of the day with Akanksha, understanding the details of the project and defining timelines for various stages. We even went out for lunch.

Akanksha was the epitome of feminity, draped in, decency. She was gracefully dressed in a cream saree. She was a beautiful girl; her almond-shaped eyes had always caught my attention. I had to accept, till the day she influenced my heart beat.

When I reached back home, I was a different man– happy and enthusiastic after a long time. Rachel wasn't back by then. I chatted with Muma for a while, diffused her concerns about my relationship with Presha.

I was upset with Presha for not calling me back on the previous day, but I also anxiously awaited a call from her that day. While I was thinking about her, I heard my phone ring, displaying Presha's name. I had always believed in telepathy. There was definitely something which was binding our souls that made us hear each other's heart even from the distance. How did Presha know I was desperately waiting for her call? I gave due credit to the waves traveling between us.

'Hey, Nightingale! How are you? Hope you are missing me?' I said.

'What's up, Adie? You seem to be flying high in the sky,' Presha's voice was vibrant.

'Yes, I'm. Crazy! I met Akanksha in the office today. We'll be working together for three months.'

'Who's she?'

'Akansha is my batch mate, once a heartthrob.'

'Hope she was, and now you have full control over your pulse,' Presha said.

'Hey! You there, you are jealous!' I was pleased with the thought.

'Not even an iota. I'll be at all times happy for you,' Presha said.

'Okay! How was your school today?'

'Good! But I missed you.

'How's everyone at home? How's Rachel?'

'Everyone is fine. Rachel is too keen to meet you.

'Can I book you for the coming weekend? We'll also get a chance to spend some time together.'

'Not now, maybe, after semester assessments.'

'Fine, let me know whenever you want to come.

'How are your babies?'

'They all are fine. When I enter the house, their eyes are looking for someone else, maybe their father.'

'Foster. I have accepted them only to make you happy. I have liked everything which came along with you, even your eccentricity,' I laughed.

'Shut up Adie! You have gone mad without me.'

'So come here soon and stay with me.'

'I'll plan on a weekend.'

'Adie, I'll call you some other time.'

'Why? Is there a knock at the door? Who can it be?'

'No Adie, it's just I need to complete my assignment for submission tomorrow.'

'You can call me anytime if you are stuck somewhere.'

'Sure Honey.'

'Bye Nightingale.'

'Bye.'

Uh! It was the first night, since our marriage, I was staying away from Presha. I missed her.

There was not much to be done. I started exploring my music collection. It was *Bryan Adams* everywhere. I was a big fan of him in my school days, even I'm till date. It's just, the craze for music had been daubed in a layer of dirt due to a busy schedule, and unraveling Presha. I smiled, looking at a CD in my hand. I was mesmerized of the day I eloped with Presha on a bike. Her eyes made her life an open book. They were clear like crystals; anyone could have peeped through to know her real self. She was true-blue.

I was perplexed by the startling change in her. I still adored her, and could never imagine a life without her. I wanted my true Presha back. I played the song "'This thing called love I just cann't handle it...............", and was lost in Nightingale thoughts.

I heard Rachel was calling me for dinner. I joined the family in the dining hall, and all through the time at the dining table I narrated the anecdotes about Macau island. Rachel was excited on my extravaganza. She wanted to know more and more about it.

Almost six weeks had gone by. On every weekend, Presha promised to visit in the next. I wanted to believe she was genuinely busy, but I was no fool. I knew she would be celebrating, having a gala time with the friends. It was frustrating. On occasions, I screeched after talking to her. The girl whose honesty, you could have sworn by had suddenly turned perjurer.

I was determined to expose the truth. Presha couldn't beguile me anymore.

I called up a private investigation agency in Singapore. I entrusted to them with the task of monitoring Presha's activities for two weeks. I asked them to keep a careful check on her friends, Mike, and Yuvi. God knew I was putting my neck under the sword. I couldn't live with a lady who was cheating on me and had different interests. On the other side, life seemed impossible without her.

At times, life puts you in a spot where you can only pray to Almighty to augment your heart beats. With folded hands, I was waiting these days to pass by.

Akanksha was the sole source of support to me. No longer, I felt I could lean on Muma's shoulders for assurance. Muma never had a high opinion about Presha. I wasn't ready to accept my defeat in front of her.

I hadn't shared anything with Akansha about Presha. I wanted to experience only positive moments with Aki. I was spellbound by the way she was handling her professional and personal life. I could see, she was progressing well in her career, and also she was a proud mother of a year old girl.

Presha and I should have planned a family too. It could have given her the much-needed stability, which is usually required for such vacillating minds.

I was anyways perturbed and that got reflected in my behavior at home.

Rachel sat with me in the living room on Sunday evening. We were planning to go out for a movie.

Her phone rang twice, but she didn't attend it. When it buzzed the third time, she disconnected it. I got too uncomfortable, and I had a hunch that she was hiding something from us.

'Why don't you pick up the phone for God sake,' I yelled at Rachel.

'It's not important?' Rachel was nervous.

'Who's calling?' I said, biting my lips, and hands tight-fisted.

'A friend,' Rachel said, with wrinkles on the forehead and eyes stuck on the ceiling.

I snatched the phone from her. It was password protected.

'Enter the password,' I ordered Rachel with the absolute authority of a big brother.

'You are crossing your limits, Adie. It's none of your business.'

'If you don't enter the password I'll break the phone,' I slapped her.

Rachel was quiescent for a moment. Her eyes turned red and her cheeks had a trail of pearls, pearls slipping in a hurry. She took the phone and entered the password.

She yelped, 'I'm ashamed of you. How can you be my brother?' and she handed over the phone to me.

'All the calls are from Kabir. Who's he?' I said, twisting Rachel's arms.

Rachel broke loose her arms and pushed me forcefully away from her, 'Damn it! He's my boyfriend, and very soon we are getting married.

'Don't you dare to interfere in my personal life, otherwise,' Rachel's face was red and her forehead was wet.

'What? You'll do anything for him, you can even kill me.'

Muma and Papa rushed into the living room where two of us were fighting like animals.

Papa immediately hugged Rachel as she was crying.

Muma stared at me, incensed, 'What has happened, Adie? Why are you out of sorts this time?

'Is this the way to behave with your younger sister?' Muma said, running her hand through Rachel's hair.

'When it comes to Rachel, you aren't my mother anymore.' I wish I could have cried.

'Stop behaving like a kid, Adie. What's your problem with her?'

'Do you know she has a boyfriend? And she's planning to marry that libidinous.'

'Mind your words, Adie!' Rachel shouted.

'Yes, I know Kabir very well. They were together in school. He's a decent guy,' Muma said, raising a finger at me.

'Oh! She's doing all this with your support. Fine! You wait and watch. She's going to ruin this family.'

'Enough, Adie! You stop this nonsense now,' Papa was furious.

I left the room and moved out of the home. I went to a bar. I thought of calling my local friends, but then I avoided facing anyone in that troubled state. I wanted to forget myself. Adie was cracking internally, there were huge voids, but not visible to anyone outside. My wife was cheating on me, and my little sister was going to ruin our family. There was no way I could have stopped anyone.

After the bar was closed, I sat at a city bus stop the whole night. The noise of traffic and beams of head- lights woke me up. I looked at my watch, it was 5 a.m. I checked my phone and there were no missed calls. Even my parents had moved away from me. Anyways, I had no option but to go back to a place which used to be my home till a day back.

My father opened the door, without looking at me he moved back to his room. He seemed so indifferent. I took forty winks and left for the office at nine o'clock.

I was a little late for the office. But then it was okay, I was an external consultant and there weren't any defined timings for me. As I entered the hall, I met Akanksha,

'Good morning, Adie! Is everything ok? You look exhausted.'

'Yeah, I'm absolutely fine,' I said, avoiding any further discussion.

'Great! Would you like to join me for the breakfast?'

'Oh! Sure. I'll take a minute to sign in, and then I'll see you in the cafe.'

Aki was waiting for me there. She was engrossed in her thoughts.

'Hey,' I said, disturbing her focus.

'Oh! Come Adie. I was waiting for you. What should I order?'

'A Chicken sandwich and coffee.'

Akanksha moved to the counter to place the order. She ordered a bread omelet for herself. Akanksha was a lovely girl; her life seemed uncomplicated unlike mine, which was drowned in troubles.

'Adie, you look upset,' she said, placing the plates on the table.

'I'm all right,' I said, stealing my eyes from her.

'It's quite visible on your face. If you don't want to share, it's up to you.'

'It's a small issue; I don't understand why it's bothering me so much.'

'My sister is involved with someone, and I have a hunch that her act is going to ruin our family.'

'It's not that I don't trust her, but she's always been soft with guys which I'm sure is going to put her in trouble.'

'How old is she?'

'Twenty-six.'

'Adie, why are we even talking about it?'

'I'm her elder brother; she's my responsibility as well.'

'She's an adult. She can take her own decisions. Moreover, I hope your parents are there to take care of her if she needs it.'

'Akanksha, it doesn't work like that.'

'Adie, if you never came close to girls doesn't mean everyone should run away from the opposite sex.'

'Even you are married now, and that too, to a girl of your choice.'

'I'm responsible, and moreover, I'm a guy.'

'Gauche! You are educated and independent. How can you be so narrow-minded?'

'Every other girl in the college had a crush on you, you know why?'

'I was a hunk. BTW, I was very comfortable with the fairer sex, but I have always defined my boundaries.' Aki preferred to ignore my last remark.

'No! It was due to the aura of intelligence and freedom around you. We all were intellectuals there.'

'Ha! Did you also like me?'

'Yaaa...I was also one of them,' Akanksha's face was red.

'You have made my day,' I blushed.

After a few minutes of silence,

'Let's get back to the work,' said Akanksha.

We were embarrassed. We got so much swayed by our tête-à-tête that we even lost our focus on Rachel's problem. Anyways, there was no point in discussing it with Akanksha.

Concentrating on work that day was difficult. A lot was going on in mind, I was restless. I invited Akanksha for lunch. She agreed to the proposal, might be, because of the turbulent state I was in. Whatever it might be, the truth was, two of us were committed to our spouses.

We had a good time together. I derived solace from Aki, the magic which was once played by Presha. I didn't try to curb my feelings. Presha was unfaithful to me; I could have never drooped to her level, but at least, I had a right to be happy.

I went back home, felt a bit refreshed. There was a guy in the living room with Rachel and Muma. Muma introduced him as Kabir, Rachel's friend. He seemed a decent man, but too meek for Rachel.

It could be a calculated choice made by Rachel. She would have never liked to be with an assertive personality. She always wanted to live in her own ways, sans any restrictions.

I waited for Kabir to go. The moment he stepped out of the house, I shared my thoughts with Rachel.

'You are a sick man. It's enough of your nonsense!' Rachel said crying.

'I'm only saying, what you are trying to do. If you are so honest, then why are you crying?'

'You have made my life hell, and I don't want to see you anymore,' Rachel said, wiping the snot with her hand.

Muma heard Rachel crying, she came rushing into the living room. She didn't give me a chance to explain my viewpoint.

'Adie, I'm sorry son, you'll have to stay at some other place. Rachel will not go anywhere, she's still our responsibility. Once she is married, you can come back anytime. It's your home,' Muma said, turning her eyes away from me.

I was paralyzed for a moment. My Muma was turning me out of the house and that too without any fault of mine. I knew Rachel more than anyone else, and in the best interest of everyone I was trying to tell her something which she might not have even realized.

Nothing was left for me in that home. Without saying any word, I picked up my luggage and exited the place. I checked into a hotel.

I was trembling; it felt like my entire energy had been drained out. I had lost appetite. I was like a corpse that lay in the bed, for others to identify and cremate. There was no one to understand my feelings, the one whom I could have trusted too. Even on the second day, I didn't get off the bed. So much so that I didn't care to inform anyone about my absence from the office.

Akanksha's phone pulled me up in the evening. I assured her of my presence in the office for the following day. The financing of their new project was dependent on approval from my end. She was interested if I could give my go ahead within the week. Aki was dedicated to her work; she wasn't used to missing any deadlines. I respected her sincerity and promised to support her.

Muma called me at night.

'How are you, Adie?'

'I'm fine. What about you and papa? How's Rachel?'

'We are fine, but Rachel is disturbed.'

'Muma, she's grown up and she needs to mend her ways now.'

'Adie, son, let her destiny take care of her. She's a sensible and matured girl. I have full faith in her.'

'At times, I feel it's only because of you, she has considered me wrong. You have without fail, shielded her every act.'

'It's over protective attitude for your sister, that you two have always been on tenterhooks.'

'I suggest you shouldn't meet her till she gets married. I hope things will change after that. There'll be someone else to take care of her.'

'Kabir is a simple guy; he can't look after her. I'm telling you she's planning to exploit him.'

'Adie, she's your sister. You shouldn't let such nasty thoughts haunt your mind.'

'Muma, she'll bring shame to our family.'

'Don't try to drive the life, Adie. A few things should be better left to the Almighty. Whatever is destined is going to happen.'

'I think it's a shallow thinking. Muma, you are a tough lady, how can you sound so helpless?'

'Adie, I'm trying to be a human being who is also a mother. Relax, and let life take its own course.

'You focus on your life. Take good care of Presha.'

'I'll try, but I can't shirk away from my responsibility.'

'Son, I think, you need a change now. High time you should pack your bags from here, and be with Presha. She must be missing you.'

'Okay, Muma, there's another call coming from Singapore. I'll talk to you some other time. You take care.'

'Bye sonny.'

I attended the call in waiting. I knew it was from the detective agency.

'Adie!'

'Hello Sir, there's a good news.'

'Yeah, tell me, I desperately need to hear something positive.'

'Sir, your wife doesn't have any extramarital affair. Most of the time she's in her college, and in the evenings she's frequently found with her classmates Yuvi and Mike; though, she spends more time with Mike.'

'Damn it, that bastard!'

'Sir, their relationship is purely platonic.'

'How do you know?'

'That's our job to know it,' guy tried to sound jovial.

'Thanks. Don't follow her anymore.'

'Fine. Bye, Sir.'

'Bye.'

I wanted to believe what he said, but I knew Presha was far more intelligent than anyone else in this world to let them know about her internal life. Anyways, I felt relaxed after hearing him.

I called up Presha. She was excited to hear my voice. I told her that my trip could be shortened by a fortnight. She was ecstatic. After talking to her, I always felt she truly loved me. I needed to trust her.

After a busy yet rejuvenating evening, I was hungry. I ordered my favorite food and red wine.

Meanwhile, I pampered myself in the Jacuzzi as I felt grubby after lying in the bed for the whole day.

Life looked much better. Butter chicken was delicious as usual, but I didn't enjoy it without Presha. Presha was the one who added savor to everything in my life. Her eyes were more stimulating than the red wine I held in my hand. Oh! I missed her.

A thought flashed in my mind to fly back to Presha for a day on the first available flight. I wanted to meet her.

I dialed an agent for ticket booking, but then the promise I made to Aki a few hours back forced me to hung up the phone. I cursed my inability.

Lost in Presha's thoughts, I lay in the bed. Sounds of springtime woke me up in the morning. The desire of being with Presha as soon as possible gave me the oomph to reach the office before time.

Aki's dedication stumped me; she was already working in the office. She supported me every bit to complete the report on time. By Friday afternoon, I sent the final report along with my approval for the project.

Akanksha came to my cubicle to invite me to dinner. At that time, I wasn't in a frame of mind to think anything beyond Presha. I had to apologize as I had booked my tickets to Singapore for the same day; I wanted to be back in the hotel to do the packing. In between I also planned to buy a solitaire for Presha. I was looking forward to a new beginning with her.

I bought a one Carat Marquise shaped solitaire ring from *Tribhovandas jewelers*. I smiled at the thought of igniting her flamboyance. It was punishing to wait anymore to see a sparkling smile on Presha's face.

I rushed back to the hotel. I called up Muma once I was through with the packing. She insisted me to visit the home before leaving for the airport. I wasn't in a mood to enter into any sort of controversy, so I didn't go there. I asked Muma not to share my program with Presha if she called up. I wanted to give her a surprise.

14th Nov 2009, Saturday 6.00 a.m.: I landed at Singapore airport. Within an hour, I was outside my apartment, excited to amaze Presha.

When I reached near the main door, I heard the voices from inside. Presha was talking to someone, a male. I had a splash of sweat, and with shaking hands, I opened the lock. Presha was standing beside the door with Yuvi, as if she was about to move out with him. Presha turned pale on seeing me. My eyes were burning, and I could feel the goose bumps.

Before I could react, 'Hey, Adie! What a pleasant surprise!' Presha said, clinging to me.

'What the hell is happening here?' I shrugged my shoulders; and pushed her back.

Presha lost her balance, and she fell on the floor. Yuvi promptly bent down, extending his hand to lift her.

I kicked his arm and grabbed him by his neck. He looked at me with hatred, clasped my hands and shoved me on the door. I pulled in my luggage and closed the door to avoid catching neighbor's attention.

My fists were clenched, and it was impossible to control my rage by any scale of rationality. I thwacked him on his face, pushing him on the ground. He fell beside Presha, and the sight of two lying together on the floor infuriated me. Then I played one sided one-two with him until he was beaten down to death. Presha beseeched for a chance to explain her side of the story. I was berserk. I dragged Yuvi to the elevator and dumped him inside it.

I came back to the apartment, locked the door from inside.

Presha was sitting on the couch with her head slightly lowered, clamped between her hands.

The Pet's squeaked; they were mourning the death of our relationship. I picked up a paperweight from the study table and smashed it on the bunny. Blood spurted from the tiny creature, and Presha's foot was colored in red. There was dead silence in the room for a second. Presha turned hysterical at the sight of annihilation.

'You! Son of a bitch! What have you done?' Presha shouted.

'You are a slut! You don't deserve to be in my house,' I said.

'Anyways, who wants to stay with you now? You are worse than a beast.'

'Filthy woman, you have used me all these years; and now I'm a junk. I'll not let you go so calmly,' I looked around, and immediately took off a badminton racket hanging on the wall. I whacked her with it.

'Adie, stop it! Otherwise, I'll call the police.'

'I'll not leave you capable of doing it,' I was ferocious. I kept spanking her.

Presha turned blue and fell unconscious on the ground. For a split second, I thought she was dead, but she was breathing. I pulled her on the bed. I took her mobile phone and alternate house keys in my custody so that she was unable to get in touch with anyone or go out of the house. I even disconnected the intercom. I wanted to isolate Presha from this world.

Soon I realized my act was barbaric, but so was Presha's behavior. She had become a floozy.

Still, I was ready to forgive her if she mended her ways. But to make that happen, she shouldn't have been allowed to move out of the house or to talk to anyone. It would be only till she regained her sanity. I was prepared to kill Yuvi and Mike if they ever tried to get in touch with her. I was all set to shift back to India if it helped me to expel these swines out of Presha's mind.

There was a beep on my phone, it was an unknown number. I picked up the phone,

'Immediately open the door or I'll call the police,' said the voice.

'Who's that?' I panicked as Presha was critical, and I would have been easily behind the bars if somebody had informed the police.

'Mike.'

'What's your problem, Mike? Wait there, I'm coming downstairs to meet you,' I was determined to thrash him, once he enters the apartment.

When I went there, I saw that he had come along with two hooligans. I didn't have any choice but to let them in.

'Mike, what are you doing here?'

'I want to meet Presha.'

'Sorry! She's sleeping.'

Mike shoved me to the ground, snatched the keys in my hand and rushed towards the elevator along with the guys.

By the time I reached back, Mike was already holding Presha in her arms. It again reminded me of the day when Presha entered my life, I was holding her in my arms, in the same way, when I brought her to my hotel room in an unconscious state. That day, the man whom I hated the most in this world was holding insentient Presha and was taking her away from me. I felt groggy; I couldn't do anything to stop her.

The rage in the eyes of the guys warned me of the possibility of any terrible incident with me at the instant.

I stood there with a bent head, avoiding to look at Presha. But the turbulence visible on the face of Mike confirmed all suspicions in my mind about his relationship with Presha. He was deeply in love with her.

'Hey, man! I'm not a great human being like Yuvi; he's lying in my home struggling for his life, but you are still safe as he regards you for being Presha's husband.

'But I'm going to quell you if you even dare to look at me or Presha from now on,' said Mike.

'Shut up! You leech! I'm letting you go out 'cause Presha wants it; otherwise, you are too small a fry for me,' I said shunning off Mike.

'Guys, I think he needs to be taught a lesson,' said Mike to his goons.

He moved out carrying Presha in his arms, banging the door behind with his foot; and his boys pulverized me till I was almost dead.

I called up my doctor friend and pleaded him for help. He did come, but his advice tasted bitter than a pill.

'Adie, there's no point dragging a relationship where you have lost the trust.

'And if you feel Presha is no longer interested in you, all the more there's a reason to let her go her own way.

'My friend, I have given you every possible treatment; but I tell you, you must visit a psychiatrist without delay.

'Call me anytime. Bye.'

'Bye.'

He was gone, but his words hounded me all throughout. I lay in the bed for two weeks. In between, only once I moved out and that too, to the doctor's clinic to get the dressing changed.

I didn't know how to get in touch with Presha since her phone was in my possession. She had changed the password of her cell, so I was unable to retrieve Yuvi or Mike's contact details.

In despair, I called up Charlie.

'Charlie, I'm ruined. Presha has left me.'

'Where has she gone?'

'I told you she's an affair. Her one of the inamorato took her from my home. I stood there like an impotent,' I yelled.

'I have failed to understand anything. Let me call Presha.'

'You can't call her. She's left her phone at home, and I don't know where she is now.'

'Adie, I'm coming there,' and Charlie hung up the phone.

I wanted to meet Presha at any cost. She had no right to leave me in limbo. I planned to go to her school. When I reached there, I was told that she hadn't attended college for several days. I got concerned about her well being. I had no option but to request them to send a message to Yuvi.

Yuvi came along with Mike to meet me.

'Hey, guys!'

'What brings you here?' asked Mike.

'I'm here to meet Presha.'

'Presha doesn't want to see your face,' said Mike.

'You better mind your own business. Where's she? I want to meet her once.'

'She's staying with me, and if you even try to get in touch with her, I'll tell you what I can do,' said Mike, raising his finger on me. He pulled Yuvi, and two of them moved inside. I stood powerless, gazing at them as they turned their backs toward me.

I decided that I wouldn't go back to work till I sort out with Presha. I went back to the apartment. I became alcoholic those days. Doubts raised by conscious mind were nagging the subconsciousness. I wanted to get rid of the vicious circle of right or wrong.

Next day, 7:00 a.m.: Charlie was outside apartment building. He called me to open the door.

'Hey buddy,' Charlie hugged me.

'Good, you came,' I said with a light hug. I could feel the warmth in our relationship had desiccated. I might be the culprit for the change.

'What has happened to you? Did you meet an accident?'

'Oh, God! Damn it! Otherwise, do you think I took a hammer to strike myself?'

'Adie, don't be so upset. Everything can be sorted out.'

'No, I don't think this can be. Presha's suitor, beat me like a hog, and took her away.'

'What Presha was doing?'

'She crossed her limits, so I gave her a piece of my mind this time– she called my mother a bitch.'

'Presha can never be so filthy.'

'Charlie, I'm not going to share anything with you, I still love her more than my life. Go and find out for yourself how crummy she can be.'

Charlie immediately left the place without even caring to look at me. He went to Presha's school. Incidentally, Presha was entering the campus as he reached there. Presha was with Mike. She was in tears to see Charlie there. It was hard for Charlie to find his Lil sister in a pathetic state. He hugged her.

Mike took them to the campus cafeteria. Presha refused to share anything with Charlie, except she informed him that she was breaking up with me. Charlie tried his best to talk to her and convince her to go home once, but Presha like her usual self was adamant on her stance and refused to discuss about me.

Charlie was leaning when he came back. His lips were pressed and eyes were hollow. There were wrinkles all across his face. It looked as if he had lived an age in two hours. I didn't need words from him to know that it was all over. His anxiety told me everything.

'Adie, Presha isn't going to come back.'

'I told you she's no longer interested in me. Nowadays, Mike is her heartthrob, and who knows, maybe, he's also a stopgap.'

'Who knows if she's been traumatized by you? Marks on her face were whimpering of protest, but she preferred to be quiet.'

'Charlie you have every right to support your sister.'

'Adie, I'm only trying not to support something visibly wrong. You shouldn't have lost your control. It's inhuman.

'Rest it's between husband and wife. You guys understand your dynamics better than anyone else.

'I'm not here to support anyone.

'Now my only request to you will be, at least, part of gracefully. Two of you have shared some of the best times in your lives; I always want you to cherish those memories.

'I plan to go back by next available flight. If you think I can be of any use to you, do call me.

'Bye.'

I stood there watching him go. I had messed up all my relationships. I knew, though, Charlie didn't blame me for anything directly, but he was aggrieved by my act.

I wanted to get back Presha at any cost. Every day in the morning I stood outside her school, to get a chance to talk to her, and waited for her till evening. One day, I got an opportunity to meet her, but she never spoke to me; and then Mike was always there with her like a shadow, eager to shun me.

I was unmoved by her behavior as I was determined to get her back. I was ready to put everything at stake for Presha. I had even stopped communicating with my office.

On our Anniversary, 2nd Dec, when I came back home in the evening, I was petrified to see the divorce notice from

Presha in the mailbox. At that Moment, I realized that all those days I had been trying to fire the ashes. It was all destroyed.

Next two days, I closed myself in the apartment, reliving the gone by years with Presha. I convinced myself for a mutual separation if Presha wanted so. Moreover, what Charlie told me had the gist of life. Presha gave a new dimension to my life, and without fail, I would have liked to cherish her memories. I couldn't have compelled her to love me. I preferred to quit.

Before it got too late, I thought of saving whatever was left in my life. I reached the office the next day. No one was delighted to see me. On the other end, I was called by our Managing Director who asked me to resign on the pretext of negligence. The project I had evaluated for financing had fudged data used for computations. I had relied on Akanksha for figures, and she manipulated everything to get the project cleared. She was promised a promotion to the post of CFO if she got it through. I was ashamed of myself, and my judgment about the people. I had always appreciated her professionalism, but ironically nowadays professionalism is sans ethics.

Chapter 8

Every corner of life left a bad taste in my mouth. I decided to go back to India. I called up Muma to share the news with her. She was exhilarated to welcome me back, but asked me to make separate arrangements for accommodation till the time Rachel was staying with them. Anyways, I also wanted to be alone for some time. At least, until the time I gave a new direction to my life.

I rented an apartment in *Gurgaon*, 25 miles away from my parent's place.

30th Jan 2010, Saturday 10:55 p.m.: I landed back in India. However, it was different Adie. I was a dejected lot.

I went to Gurgaon straightaway. It was a beautiful large setup on the sixth floor. I wanted to be in a secluded place like the one, away from inquisitive eyes. As I entered the apartment, a melancholy feeling set in me. I missed Presha. I played her favorite song, opened a bottle of vodka; her bold eyes were staring at me from the veil of hair falling over her face.

I lay in bed till the next day. Muma called me up. She asked me to visit the home. Besides fervor, there was urgency in her voice. I was afraid if Charlie had talked to her. Anyways, one day she would have known everything.

I hired a cab, and reached, my once upon a time sweet home, at 6:00 p.m.

Moms always make you feel important; and their presence, even it might be for a short duration, helps you forget any predicament you are in.

Papa and Rachel also waited for me. I was relaxed to find everyone around.

Rachel was happy to see me, and so was Papa. In her usual style, she embraced me. I, too, tightly hugged her, and tears from my eyes couldn't stop from shedding. I wished if I could give all the happiness to my sister. I had always loathed to see her distressed; it turned me crazy. However, the irony was, I had been the cause of many of her troubles. I couldn't stop being protective of her, as eternally, I had a hunch that she was a debauched girl, and one day she would bring shame to our family.

Muma asked me if everything was okay, she had never seen me that emotional. Everyone was keen on meeting Presha. It was a relief to know that they weren't aware of the reality. I pretended that Presha was busy with her classes, and she would join me after her final exams.

I shared tea with the family in the living room. Muma broke the news of Rachel's wedding with Kabir on the coming Saturday. Kabir and Rachel had been doing the arrangements. They had planned a grand affair at *The Taj*. Muma asked me to invite my friends, and she had already called up Presha's family. Presha's father wasn't keeping well, so they hadn't confirmed their presence.

I was excited for Rachel, but then a sulky feeling was creeping in– if everything would go as planned.

By the time, we finished our dinner it was midnight. Muma asked me to stay back for a day. It was anyways, challenging to fake even for a few hours gone by, staying there would have meant revealing everything; at least, to my mother. I was already biased for Rachel; it wasn't opportune for me to do or say anything which she didn't like, howsoever true it might be. I insisted on going back.

Although, it was late at night, I called up Charlie while on my way back. He was surprised to know that I was back in India. He didn't ask me about Presha, which was enough for me to know that he was in touch with Presha. I wasn't sure what all Presha had disclosed to him.

'Charlie, Presha sent me a divorce notice.'

'I know.'

'Why didn't you inform me that she was planning on those lines, and why the hell you didn't stop her?'

'She told me only after she had sent it; moreover, she didn't seek any advice from me,

'Adie, you know how Presha is!'

'If she has taken a decision, it's final.'

'Who can know her better than me; she's the most stubborn person on this earth.'

'It's not the question of her attitude this time. It's something much deeper. She's genuinely hurt.

'She's tight-lipped, and that's, what has baffled me.'

'Is she still staying with Mike?'

'Yep, I offered her to move with Priyanka, but she refused.'

'Charlie, things are crystal clear. She's a whore. After spoiling my life, she's having a gala time with that creepy stalker, Mike.'

'Adie I can't hear such nasty remarks for Presha. I know she's a great girl.'

'I'm her husband, so I know her better than you. I have seen her stooping down to the level of gazing waiters in a restaurant, flirting with my friends, and now this, Yuvi, and Mike.'

'Charlie, please don't defend her. I want her back 'cause I love her; otherwise, I have no confusions about her.'

'Adie, if you are so sure about her, then let her go gracefully. There's no point dragging this relationship if you don't trust her anymore. ***Love without trust is like a myth.***'

'Okay! If she wants to go, let her. I hope it makes you happy.

'Charlie, you are my best buddy and will always remain so.'

'Two of you are equally important to me; I love you both.'

'I know. BTW I called you to inform that Rachel's wedding is on this Saturday; you are anyways coming. And, I haven't shared anything about Presha with Muma. Maybe I'll, after the wedding is over.'

'I understand. I'm going to be there as your friend and not as Presha's brother.'

'I'll wait for you. Good night.'

'Bye.'

I drew away from people. Most of the time, I lay in the apartment with music on; and red wine, trying to do some magic on my mind.

I was calling Muma every now and then to ask if I could be of some help to her. She always told me that as such there wasn't any work for me, but my presence at home would anytime be a pleasure for them.

I was fully aware that my family didn't have any hidden treasures, and I'll have to start working soon to pay the bills. I postponed it till the wedding.

Charlie didn't turn up until Saturday morning. I wasn't complaining as he had every reason for not being there. I didn't even call him; it would have embarrassed him.

Muma called up to know when I was coming home. It was high time for me to put back depression and act like an elder brother whose sister was getting married that day. I looked into the mirror; an unkempt beard and hair horrified me. Adie, who was known for his styles, was lost in the layers of time.

I went to the salon to get back in shape. I could manage it reasonably well.

Stretched lips and raised cheeks of my parents welcomed me to the wedding.

My parents were busy greeting guests at home while I was asked to reach the venue to check the arrangements.

It was a well-managed affair. Rachel and Kabir had planned everything in such minute details, that there was hardly anything, which required attention.

Muma and Papa, arrived at the venue at 7:00 p.m., along with some other members of our first family. Barat (Marriage procession) had arrived, but Rachel wasn't seen around until 9:00 p.m. I was perturbed. I knew something wrong was going to happen. I was desperately trying to contact Rachel, but the other side always repeated that she wasn't still ready.

Kabir and his parents were taking it in a stride. They were busy meeting our family, and Kabir's eager eyes were looking through the entry gate to get a glimpse of his bride.

I was sweating, clutching my fingers and pacing like a pendulum outside the main gate. "There!" Her car arrived. It stopped at me, and Rachel opened the door. She was looking majestic, an angel. I felt getting back my heart beat. I wished if my fears about her were evaporated that day.

I took her to a room before she walked down the aisle. As per the ritual, she was to walk beneath a veil of flowers held by the brothers at the four corners. I along with my two cousins held the veil, but we realized still one more person was required. Before I could ask anyone to be a part of this ritual, I saw Charlie standing there with the fourth end in his hand. That time I could feel the blood flowing through my veins. With a smile on my face, we started the procession, and Rachel walked down the aisle in grandeur.

The marriage was solemnized. Rachel left with Kabir to start a new life. I felt light as is if some burden had been taken off me.

Next day, Charlie took the morning flight to Kolkata. We hardly got a chance to talk. Anyways, there wasn't much left between us to be shared.

Muma insisted that I should shift back to their home, but I was inclined to be alone for some time. I went back to Gurgaon the same day. I thought I would be alone there, but memories of lovely time with Presha didn't leave me even for a second.

Before I left Singapore, Mike collected Presha's stuff from the apartment, including her pets. However, what he couldn't take away from me was the sparkles of her eyes, which lighted my life when I closed mine; the music of her breath, which flowed into my ears when I was lonely; and waves of her touch, dripping on the sand of my body.

"Presha, why did you leave me? I could have changed everything to make you happy.

"If you are ready to do anything to make her happy, and if she wants freedom from you, give it to her. Perhaps, she'll be happy."

I immediately signed the divorce papers and sent them to Mike's address. Though bleak, I had a hope that Presha would never use them.

I had tumbled down from a cliff. I didn't know how to manage life on the ground. I abhorred the idea of going out to find a job, but there was no option. I had nil savings as I had spent everything in the extravaganza with Presha. To top it all I had promised to pay her school fee, still one more year was to go.

I met the top consultants in Delhi, and they assured me of the quick response.

Within no time, I had two excellent opportunities in hand, and I preferred to join as a Director in a commercial finance unit of an American bank.

I had been talking to my parents on the phone all these days, but never visited their home. I hadn't yet shared about the turbulence going on in my life with them, I couldn't muster the courage to face them with the heart-shattering reality of my life. At least, now I was back in a job, and a bit stabilized. I went to meet them over a weekend.

Rachel was visiting home along with Kabir and her brother-in-law, over lunch. I reserved disclosure of my reality to Muma and Papa after her visit.

Kabir was a charming boy, and so was his brother. They were looking a nice happy family. I was delighted for Rachel.

Somehow, I observed Rachel paying undue attention to her brother-in-law. At times, unnecessarily she would embrace him, another time she would run her fingers through his hair. The boy seemed to be embarrassed by the act of her's. Her behavior was repulsive.

I held Rachel's hand and dragged her to my room.

'I have told you several times to behave decently with the opposite sex.'

'Adie, what are you saying? I don't understand.'

'I'm referring to your lecherous actions with your brother-in-law. He's abashed, aren't you feeling ashamed?'

'What nonsense are you saying? He's like my younger brother.'

'He's like, but he's not your brother.'

Rachel started crying. On hearing her voice, Kabir swiftly moved in. He embraced her and started kissing on her forehead.

'What has happened, Rachel? Why are you crying?'

'Kabir, let's go from here.'

'Yeah, sure we'll go, but tell me what made you cry?'

'Nothing.'

'Rachel, I know you very well. You won't cry over nothing. Tell me if I can help you in sorting out anything.'

'Yes! You can help in mending her flirtatious nature. I would have killed my wife if she had behaved like a slut with my brother,' I said.

Kabir walked towards me, waited for a moment; slapped on my face with the ultimate strength to turn it into an apple.

He held Rachel's hand and moved out of the room without even turning around once. I was amazed to find the cutie pie turning into a Tarzan.

I knew I wasn't meeting Rachel after it. But, I prayed to God to save Rachel from Kabir's wrath, once he realized his wife's truth.

Muma and Papa were extremely upset with me; they didn't say it, but their eyes told me to get out of the house without any further delay. I didn't react, I immediately moved out from there.

I came back to my apartment feeling all the more lonely. Gradually, all my relationships had slipped out of my hand, leaving me alone, like a man stranded on a remote island in the mid of a sea.

I was alone, but still a bleak hope of Presha returning back to me had never abandoned me.

I joined the new office. I wasn't enjoying it at all, but you need to do something to survive. I wish if the Almighty, would have created a social dole system for his not so rich kids. When he can create a complex entity like a human being, he could have done anything if he wished so. Anyways, I wasn't in a state to deliberate with God on what he could have done better.

I started working on my mundane job; Nikki became the biggest relief in my life, though, she was my personal assistant, but she acted as a spiritual guru too. With her, I realized a different meaning of life—*life is nothing but a bundle of events, some you might call as pleasant surprises and others as shocks. But every event contained in the bundle of life*

has to unfold, it's up to you, whether you enjoy the passing by of shock as it has lightened the weight of your bundle, or you even forgo the joys of pleasant surprises because of it, thus making your bundle heavier.

Nikki's life was difficult. She had separated from her husband 'cause he was an alcoholic. He had made her life wretched. She struggled for five years trying to change him, but when he became a threat to her son, she had no choice except to leave him. She had been pleading him for the divorce, but he was harassing her for more money.

I felt sad for the girl. She was so caring and patient. She had always believed in the goodness of human beings– people who can be bought or sold for some printed papers. I was disgusted. But then in the words of Nikki, her pleasant surprises were still to unfold.

I could see in the mirror, stress had been brutal to me. The pale glowing skin developed splashes of darkness; bold, sparkling eyes shrank as if they were shy of facing the light. Adie had lost his charm.

It was time for Presha's third-semester fee payment. I transferred the money to her bank account, only to find a reverse transfer in my account the next day. I was anticipating it. Presha was an egoistic girl; she would have never accepted anything from me. Moreover, now Mike was there to take care of her needs.

Next day, while I was going to the office, I received a call from Presha's lawyer informing me about the hearing in *Tis Hazari* court after two months.

My only ray of hope was gone. When Nikki saw me, she could assess the terrible state I was in. I shared with her the reason of turmoil. She innocently held my hand and nodded with her eyes, as if she was asking me to wait till the event unfolds. She told me that Presha might change her mind after seeing me. But I knew she was an obstinate girl who won't yield to anything in life, but still I wanted to believe Nikki.

I started spending more and more time with Nikki, it gave me the much-needed comfort. Beyond a time she wasn't available for me, she was a dedicated mother too. After six o'clock it was only his son in her mind, and I respected her for the woman she was.

* * * * *

The day arrived when I was to appear in the court along with Presha. Dew drops were spread all across my face. My heart was thumping fast. I was seeing Presha after six months. I didn't know how would I come back if the day decides not to turn in my favor, I was sure it would be four men carrying me back.

I requested Nikki to accompany me to the court. She told me to face it boldly and happily; in any either way, I would be lightening the bundle.

I knew, I wasn't that strong, but I didn't have any choice but to face it.

I reached the court at 10:00 a.m.; Presha came five minutes later. Mike wasn't there, she came with her lawyer.

I was shocked to see her. She looked frail. Her two eyes looked like deep valleys surrounded by dark clouds. Her long hair was tied in a bun, and they had lost almost half the volume. Her lips were blue showing cracks all over. I even felt as if she was slightly drunk. I could have never imagined seeing her in such a poignant condition.

I tried to approach her, but her lawyer stopped me from coming even near to her. Presha had asked him to do so; he was merely doing his job.

We appeared before the judge where Presha's lawyer expressed his client's inability to remain in the wedlock. I was paralyzed; there wasn't any point in dragging this relationship if she wasn't interested in me anymore. I gave my consent to every word told by the lawyer.

I once again looked at Presha. She was stoned. It seemed she gave a damn to whatever was happening.

We were granted divorce; decree would have taken some time to reach.

Presha didn't look at me even once; she immediately left with her lawyer after the judgment. It seemed she was eager to go back to share the news with Mike. Presha was a sincere girl if it wasn't for the bastard Mike, who maneuvered her mind.

The night was an endless tunnel. I was lost in the darkness. There was no gleam of hope. Rivers were flowing from the two oceans, and I had no control over it, but to get drowned in the flow. I couldn't believe my heart was still throbbing, what a shameless creature I was?

After some time, the outside world was lit, but I was still eclipsed. I lay in the bed brooding.

A phone call from Nikki forced me to get back to work.

I reached office in a disheveled state. Nikki wasn't there on her chair. I rushed to my cabin where I sat with crossed fingers on my lips, and my face cocked towards the door. I was anxious to meet Nikki. As soon as she arrived, my eyes turned sparkly red like a child, on seeing her. I wanted to run to her and embrace her. Rather, I stole my eyes from her and looked outside the glass wall.

'Hey, Adie! Are you okay?' Nikki said in a shaky voice.

'I have lost everything in life, Nikki,' I said, turning my moist eyes towards her. It was embarrassing to face Nikki in the shattered state.

'Relax! What happened?' Nikki's eager hands wanted to caress me, but she held back.

'We are divorced. The worst was Presha didn't even look at me, talking to her was a distant dream. The girl in my every breath, a few days back, has alienated from me so much, she doesn't even recognize me now. How is this possible, it's awful, Nikki? I have failed in life,' I said, weeping.

'Adie, you need to get hold of yourself. We are in the office. If you want, we can go to some other place.'

'Ugh! I'm okay here.'

'Adie, there's a thing called destiny, and you need to duly respect it.'

'Why it's only me?'

'I can also say the same thing. God has blessed you with all the riches of life, I'm sure you would have never asked him, "Why me?"

'Think of me, I have never seen in my life any pleasant surprise unfolding from my bundle, but still, I'm living on a hope that one day it will.

'So, it's not only you, but everyone has his share of problems which we need to embrace, and move forward,' Nikki said with a cracked voice.

'I'm not that strong.'

'You are, Adie. I'm sending some tea for you.

'I need to discuss a few issues with you before you go to the meeting scheduled after an hour.'

I moved up my head. I had never observed Nikki, it seemed. She was damn beautiful. Her bright, glowing brown eyes just radiated peace and love.

'Nikki, look how selfish, I have been. It's been a while I asked you about your case?'

'He's asking an enormous price for my freedom; my freedom isn't important, I can forgo it, but I can't sacrifice my son's life.'

'If you allow me, I can help.'

'No thank, Adie. This is my fight, and I'll handle it,' Nikki said going back to the business.

I was breathing those days as stopping it wasn't in my hands, and God was also not kind enough to grant me peace.

I wasn't doing exceptional in my professional life. I abhorred interacting with the people. Nikki was the only support I had in the office.

I was living alone in my Gurgaon apartment. I neither wanted to stay with my parents nor did they ever ask me to stay with them. Though, I had started talking to Muma over the phone, but Papa was still annoyed with me. I didn't speak to Rachel after the incident.

I called up city's best interior designer Rui Singh to make my home.

It's true; you are influenced by the company you are with.

It was Presha inside me who was doing what I was visibly executing.

After deliberations, we finalized *copper and ivory* theme for walls, furniture, upholstery, and curtains. Rui imported the crystals from the *Czech Republic* and *Ireland*. The view was a royal treat for the eyes and a big cut in the pocket.

I realized within a short span of time, the extravaganza didn't have either any material or emotional value for me, except, it kept me busy for a few days. The place lamented loneliness and harrowing experiences of life.

I didn't share about my divorce with Muma, but she had a premonition, that it was on the way. Like any other loving mother, my mother was always apprehensive about Presha's attitude towards marriage. It wouldn't be fair to say that she thought I was a perfect marriage material. She knew I had my own set of problems, that's why she wanted a docile, patient, flexible and a caring girl– a goddess, to handle me.

Nikki was the only person I could confide in. She could easily relate to me, she too was in the same state as I was in. I was getting closer to Nikki those days. I wasn't sure whether it was sympathy, or Nikki had started loving me. I dreaded to explore my feelings for her. Whatever it was, I liked the silence in our relationship.

Finally, anxiety in me had to encounter its cause– the divorce decree which was couriered to me by our lawyer. I knew it was to happen one day, but I wished that day would never come.

I had no one else to look to but Nikki. I immediately called her. It was Saturday. She invited me to her house for lunch. I had no reason to avoid it. She had a two bedroom apartment in the west of Delhi. It was a simple and cozy place, quite contrary to where I was living in, or what Presha would have wanted to be her home.

Nikki's six-year-old son was an adorable kid. But he was cowed and diffident; his father had tyrannized the family. I could feel what Nikki might have gone through. A bad marriage can be ferocious to your existence. You lose confidence in humanity when the person you considered as your soul mate lacerates your heart, for something not priced, in any way, above pure love.

Nikki hadn't shared much with me about her marriage, but, from whatever little I knew her husband was a douchebag.

Nikki didn't broach on the topic of my divorce, till the time I was there at her home. Her waxed eyes and mellowed voice reflected the pain she felt for me. It was her beauty, though, she kept a distance yet she was a panacea."

Chapter 9

I wake up by the glimmer of sunlight filtering through the glass windows. I gain consciousness by scrubbing eyes. Still not out of the dream, I roll my eyes around to find out it's not my luxurious bedroom, but office cabin where I'm lying in a chair with the lower half of my body leaning on the floor. I gain the balance and lift up myself. The clock on the wall shows six o'clock. I look at the laptop on the table; it reminds me, I have missed the VC with Brian yesterday. I see a stinker from Brian on *Sametime*. I have screwed up everything. I wish Nikki is here to take me out of the mess. My head is loaded and heart is glum; I want to run away from this world. I leave a note for Nikki– I was in the office the whole night, I'll be late today.

With a deafening silence outside; and raucousness of loneliness inside me, I open the door. I move to the bedroom and throw myself on the king size bed.

Eyes are afraid to shut down; they dread to see the life gone by. With dilated eyes stuck on the ceiling, I lie there feeling despondent.

There's a ring on my phone. I pick up the phone, not caring to see who the caller is.

'Adie!'

'Adie, what has happened to your voice?' It's Muma.

'Nothing, I'm still in the bed.' I know Muma isn't going to take my words.

'Is your health okay? Aren't you attending the office today?'

'Muma, I came from the office in the morning.'

'Why don't you look for some other job? It's quite hectic here. You are taxing your health this way.'

'No! Nikki wasn't there, and I didn't realize when I drowsed off while working.'

'Adie, son, you need to be with someone,' anxiety in Muma's voice was quite audible.

'Muma, I'm too tired for this discussion.'

'Okay! You take a rest. I'll come sometime this week to meet you.'

'Bye,' and I hang up the phone, with all the more increased levels of adrenaline.

The phone is buzzing again, and still, Muma's words are hounding me.

'Hey, Nikki.'

'Good Morning, Adie.'

'You can't be late today. Brian is furious, and he's waiting for your call.'

'I have fixed it for ten o'clock. Please be there on time,' Nikki says, sounding too professional.

'Fine. I'm coming.'

'Bye.'

'Bye.'

Perhaps, Muma is right. I need to be with someone.

There's a feeling, which I can't exactly identify, but I want to rush to the office.

I was in the office. I looked at my watch, still five minutes to go to the meeting.

'Good Morning, Nikki.'

'Can we go out for lunch today?' I'm revolting against my real self, which is stopping me from crossing my limits of decency.

'Adie, we need to be there in VC with Brian,' Nikki is zapped.

'Yeah. Of Course!

'Gimme a minute. I'll join you in the conference room.'

I drop the bag in the cabin, and within a minute I'm seated in front of the screen facing Brian. Brian looks irritated, and why not? He has every reason to be so.

'Hi Brian, I'm so sorry for yesterday; I kept you awake so late at night.'

'Adie, you know it was urgent.

'At least, you should have left a message with Nikki.

'She has no clue about you.' Brian is rebuking me as if I'm a child, and Nikki is the one who is governing my life. Maybe he's right, whenever she isn't there, I goof up the things.

'Brian, I apologize. I was in the hospital with high blood pressure. I didn't even get a chance to inform Nikki about it.' I'm a human being who needs excuses to live life with dignity.

'Oh! Adie! Please excuse me for being so insensitive.

'How are you now?'

'I'm much better.

'Our presentation is imperative. Let's do it quickly before I get a stroke,' I say with a wicked smile. Nikki looks at me perplexed.

I'm feeling rejuvenated. I flip through the slides with vigor. Brian seems impressed as he hasn't interrupted me even once during my loquacious slide show. It seems I'm emerging as a winner, and I have Brian's approval.

I say bye to Brian, and incline my face towards Nikki.

'Nikki, Will you like to go out for lunch with me?'

'Adie, is there something special? You have never ever been so generous.'

'It's very special. I need to talk to you.'

'Can we do it here?'

'No, I need individual attention from you.'

'Okay. Where should I book the table?' Nikki says it with a lopsided smile.

'Presha would have preferred to go to a bar, but let's go to some decent restaurant,' I'm embarrassed on my kiddish remark.

'Cool!'

I have never seen a broad smile like the one on her face. I can feel my remark hasn't gone too well with her either. But Nikki is an amazing lady; she'll take on the pain rather than to inflict it on someone else. She's special.

Though my eyes are stuck on the laptop, ears are eager to hear the intercom buzz.

It's twelve o'clock, Nikki calls me to inform that I should be ready to hit *Hyatt*. It's for the first time since she's been with me, she has called me *Sir*. Maybe, she wants to remind me of the relationship we have.

I follow her to the car in the parking. For an introvert guy like me, life was very comfortable with Presha as without fail, she led me, and I followed her. But it was different with Nikki, though, she was commanding when it came to work, but I can feel, she's hesitant to go out with me. I had always liked reserved females like Nikki, but I can't say how my chords struck with Presha.

We reach Hyatt, and follow our way to *Aangan*. The ambience is decent, but nothing spectacular. It's a peaceful place, which is of utmost importance to me. While Nikki is ordering the food, I'm gathering my nerves to understand why we are here. I want to share last's night anxiety with her. I'm sure there's nothing more than that on my mind.

Anyways, let me say something to her.

'Nikki, I was in the office last night. I don't know when I fell asleep. But when I woke up, I was so lonely, and I only wanted to meet you. So, we are here,' my words are having their own way. I think Presha has influenced them too.

Nikki looks at me with droopy eyes.

'Nikki, I don't know what I want from life, but I want you to be there with me.'

'What?'

'Yeah, I can't describe it, but I know I'm at ease when you're around.'

'Are you saying– you are in love with me.' Nikki can beat anyone when it comes to keeping life simple.

'No, I don't think so. I had a love marriage with Presha, the way she betrayed my faith, I dread the word *love*. I'm better off sans it. Perhaps, it's not about Presha, females in general should never be trusted."

'You don't love me, you can't believe me; what is it you're trying to tell me, Adie? This isn't you!'

'Nikki, I want you to stay with me as a friend, though, I believe you are different from other girls, yet I'm not in an emotional state that I can blindly trust you.

'I want to know what you feel for me.'

'Adie, I have always liked you; but do I want a relationship with you, is something I have never considered. I have a son to take care of, and moreover, I'm still not divorced.'

'I can take all your responsibilities. You, just be with me; you are the only one who gives solace to my life.'

'Adie, what you have just said has come out of the blue. I thought you wanted to talk to me about Presha. I'm baffled.

'Gimme some time to think about it,' Nikki said, looking in my eyes.

I'm sure, Nikki can solve any problem. She's awesome.

Every day I come to the office, to hear something positive from Nikki. I'm only living with a hope that soon she would be around to take care of my life.

Nikki is not saying anything. She takes care of her job and goes back. Her frigid behavior is bothering me.

It's Friday. I hope I can thank God for the day it is.

I reach the office, and Nikki is sitting in my cabin.

'Good morning, Nikki.'

'Morning, Adie.' Nikki steals her eyes.

I sit on a chair in front of Nikki. Even, I avoid facing Nikki. My heart thumps faster; I realize she's here to decide about my life. I inhale deeply to give some peace to my heart.

'Adie, these three days were hard on me. I have been asking myself several questions, and finding answers to them was strenuous.

'I have realized that you are governing my life since I met you.

'A smile on your face in the morning peps me up, and a wrinkle on your forehead makes me restless.

'I don't know how, but since I have known you, I think I love you.

'I'm happy to be with you in any way.'

I exhale. It's not what I want her to feel, I need to be honest. I cut loose from her feelings and say,

'Nikki but I don't love you. I just want you around.'

Now, she stares into my eyes; her elbows set on the table and her hands fidgeting in front of her chest.' I don't care what you feel; I have confided my emotions in you.

'Adie, I can't stay with you, it'll impact my divorce.

'You can stay near my apartment; that way, I can take care of you as well as my son.

'I don't need anything from you; I know how to live within my means. If possible, please love my son like yours.'

Nikki moves out of the room without giving me a look. A smile beams on my face; she's agreed to be with me.

God has been kind enough to me, though, in parts. But I can't be more grateful to the Almighty for what he has given me. I can't survive without Presha; maybe, with Nikki around, I'll be able to travel dark tunnel of life.

It takes a week to search for an apartment near Nikki's place. I'm lucky enough to get it just on the top floor of Nikki's home.

I shift to my new house. It's comparatively a smaller place than the one I'm used to. Spend on flamboyancy has gone into the drain. But I'll like to keep this place simple; Nikki is here to cut off the remains of Presha inside me.

The weird feeling of love and hatred for Presha has been torturing my mind. I know, I loathe her for what she has done to me, but why does my heart cry when I think of her.

With countless baffling thoughts, I'm leaning on Nikki for an answer.

Life is flowing like a stream within the banks of Nikki and my apartment. Though, for most of the time I'm at Nikki's place. We are living as a family, and I have become more than a real father of Karan. He's gaining confidence and is a much happier kid now.

Today, I have taken Nikki and Karan to my parents place. Papa didn't even come out of his room to meet us, but Muma was happy to meet Nikki. Nikki was exactly like the silhouette of life partner Muma had in mind for me.

Usually, we go out to the movies and shopping on weekends. Karan is thrilled to go out for a movie, with me and Nikki in the evening. It's an old movie; we can easily get a window booking.

Karan is stomping his feet and pulling Nikki's shirt. He whines for a demand, and she ignores. Karan is hesitant to talk to me directly; though, he looks at me in between but takes away his eyes as soon as I flick my head upwards. Nikki tells me that he wants an ice cream. I ask her to line up for tickets, and I take Karan for an ice cream. Karan is fond of chocolate bars, and no sooner he has one in hand, he's licking it, smearing his mouth and hands.

Nikki is standing at the window, chatting with the guy inside. She's laughing as he's saying something, and his piercing eyes are scanning Nikki.

Oh, gauche! These females don't understand how mean men can be. At least, Nikki should have known it. She has seen the world, and she is a single Mom for the last five years.

I'm irked by her behavior. She realizes that there are people lined up. She collects the tickets and moves out.

'Hey, son, how's your ice cream?' asks Nikki.

'Adie, we have the tickets; let's move fast.'

'You were at leisure when you were talking to the counter boy. What has happened to you now?'

'He was telling me how kids usually behave after watching this movie.'

'Oh! Is he a psychologist?'

'No, they watch them every day.'

'But they don't talk to everyone here. A stranger speaks to you only if he gets the loose rope.

'I understand Nikki your job demands you to be nice to everyone, but you aren't doing a job here. The guy had lust in his eyes, and you seemed to be pleased.'

'Sorry, Adie! I'll be careful in future,' Nikki tells me politely; but her eyes are unmoved, and lines are visible on her forehead.

I want to smack her, but then all females are alike.

Karan is ecstatic to be with us, watching the fantasy world. I have seen the life so closely; that howsoever I try, I can't be vivacious enough to enjoy fables.

Perhaps, I never did it, even as a child. It's only due to my affection for Karan; I'm sitting here testing my patience.

What a relief! Finally, the movie is over!

'Hey, Nikki. Is Karan behaving in the way, the other kids do?'

Nikki smiles and looks at Karan to see what he's doing. She's ignoring me; I hope she's not oblivious to what I have told her.

Nikki's lips are sealed. Her eyes are not aggrieved; they aren't weary either, but, they are apprehensive. Maybe, my words haven't gone too well with her. I find her morose.

'Nikki, let's have dinner here. It's already nine o'clock, you must be tired, don't bother to cook.'

'As you say.' She isn't pleased by the concern shown by me.

'Yeah uncle, let's go. I'm starving for French fries and a coke,' Karan says, holding my hand.

He pulls me to a nearby *McDonalds*. I look at Nikki, and she slightly nods her head. We grab burgers and a meal for Karan.

Karan is yawning and rubbing his eyes, to fight the sleep with the shutter guard. Nikki suggests calling it a day.

We reach back home. Nikki takes Karan to his room. After she puts him to bed, Nikki comes in the living area and sits beside me. Her silence is shattering my ears with countless inevitable questions.

'Nikki, say something.'

'I'm extremely sorry, Adie. I must have done something terribly wrong. I have never seen you in such anger in the past,' tears aren't stopping to shed from Nikki's eyes. She is as if telling to life, enough is enough. Another shock has unfolded for her.

'Nikki, I have always considered you a female of high esteem, I can't tolerate if people toss around you as sleazy.

'I want, you shouldn't talk to men who are strangers.'

'Adie, I'll be careful in future.'

Holding her face in my hands, I wipe off her tears and kiss her.

Sunday morning, Nikki wakes me up with a cup of tea. Her eyes are sparkling, and she blushes. I too feel the freshness of blood coursing through my veins. Nikki looks up, and our eyes meet. Her face turns a shade darker; I quickly steal my eyes, and I'm wiggling my fingers. She sets the cup on the storage headboard and moves out.

We spend the entire day at home; I'm engrossed in music, flipping through the pages of a novel. Nikki is busy with Karan. I have a yearning to be with her every time I hear her voice.

Life is gradually coming on track. Muma was so right in her assessment of my life partner. Girls like Presha can give you the fun time, but they can't be with you all the time.

Saturday is back. Weekends are fun; I'm chalking out several plans for the day. Nikki needs to finalize what she thinks the best.

Seven o'clock: There's no sound of rhymes resonating the house, Karan is sleeping. There's a drone from the kitchen, Nikki's preparing the bed tea.

I used to cook quite often with Presha. There were times when I wanted to do so, and on other occasions, it was required; otherwise, I would have starved, especially, when Presha got preoccupied in her school, minuscule like cooking dropped from her *A* list.

Next weekend, Nikki will have every meal, even bed tea, served to her. I should extend her support in running the house.

I'm busy pondering about the next week, and there she is, with a tray in her hand.

'Good morning. You look fresh!'

'Good morning, Adie. Thanks! I slept well.'

Nikki hands over a cup of tea to me. She takes a cup in her hand and sits on a couch in the room.

There's an awkward silence in the room except, made by our breath,

Phuuuuu. Hmmmmmm...

'Who made bed tea when you were with Presha?' says Nikki, with twinkling eyes.

'No set rules. We both used to do it,' her inquisitiveness startles me; or maybe she wants to tell me, I should also do something, which anyways I was thinking of.

'Adie, I know it's a sensitive topic, but I'm keen to know more about Presha.'

'No, it's fine. But, she isn't worth talking about.'

'Please, if you don't mind.'

'Okay!' I take a pause to gather my thoughts. I don't know why I do so. If I close my eyes anytime, I see Presha performing on the stage, then, what am I trying to recollect in front of Nikki.

'If it's hard for you, please let it go.'

'I saw Presha when she was performing in her college...,' I'm narrating as if I'm again living those moments with Presha, I want them to go on forever.

All of a sudden I'm doleful.

'Something wrong, Adie! Are you okay?'

'Yeah! I wish this part of life shouldn't have unfolded.

'It was her first day of the college, and I was waving her from the balcony...,' I tell her everything– my anxiety attack, Yuvi, Mike and how she dumped me.

I can see, Nikki is benumbed. 'I know Nikki, anyone will lose faith in humanity after hearing it. But this is a bitter reality of my life, and now you'll understand why I don't trust females.'

Nikki is staring at me as if her piercing eyes are clicking every expression of mine and trying to connect to the pain in them.

'Did you tell her about your feelings, or ever asked her the reason for her behavior?'

'Nikki, there was nothing to ask. She was like a river whose cardinal was to flow. I tried building a dam, which couldn't exist in the vagaries of life. She met Yuvi and Mike, who excited her more than I did.'

Nikki was quiet, but there were lines on her face, and her eyes were motionless.

'Mummy, Mummy,' Karan enters my room, rubbing his eyes. He cuddles his mother and straddles on her lap. Nikki sits there unmoved patting Karan's back and running her fingers through his hair. Karan is half asleep.

'Get up baby. It's too late.

'I'll take you to pee,' Nikki says, unfolding Karan's arms, and he slides off half on the floor and his upper half snuggling his mother's legs.

Nikki picks him up and takes him to the washroom.

I have a mixed bag of feelings. I'm restless, Presha is back with me; and on the other hand, I'm palliated to share everything with Nikki.

The day is good. I have a great time at home with my newly found family.

Monday, as usual, Nikki goes to the office by a chartered bus and I take the car. She leaves the home a little early.

When I enter the office, I see Nikki talking to a guy, he must be about my age. As I cross them in haste, I hear Nikki call out my name.

'Hey, Adie.' I turn around to face her.

'Yes, Nikki,' I say, looking straight into her eyes, avoiding the gentleman standing beside her.

'Adie, he's Dushan– our new treasury director.'

'Hey, Adie,' Dushan holds out his hand.

'Hey, how are you?' I shake hands with a bit of hesitation.

I take him to my room, request Nikki to send two cups of tea inside.

No sooner we start conversing than Nikki is there in the room along with the pantry boy who is holding the tray of teacups.

Dushan catches the eyes of Nikki, and they exchange smiles. She looks at me to ask if I'll prefer some cookies with tea. She knows I had a sumptuous breakfast in the morning, then why she's creating this fuss. I politely refuse; requesting her not to disturb me while I'm with Dushan.

I think, five minutes would have passed since Dushan had come in my room, there's beep on my intercom; it's from 101.

'Yes, Nikki.'

'Adie, a meeting is lined up for you at twelve o'clock.'

'I know that; still there's ample time,' I say, putting down the cradle.

Hardly, have we talked, Nikki is there in the room on some other pretext.

'Adie, there's an urgent mail from Brian, and he's awaiting your reply.'

'Doesn't he have something better to do in life? He has sent me an email now and he's expecting an immediate response.

'Tell him I'm involved somewhere else.'

Nikki gives a smug look at Dushan, and that idiot beams again. Perhaps, he understands Nikki is trying to catch his attention.

'Okay, Aadir, it's nice meeting you. You, please catch up with the work. I'll come some other time,' and he moves out. Nikki also follows him out of the door.

Two of them chat outside Nikki's booth. Nikki has a gleaming smile; and Dushan looks at her with a tilted face, squeezed eyes and a sly smile.

I gaze at them from the glass door. I'm remorseful of my misreckoning of Nikki. She's no different. In despair, I bend my face down, covering it with both the hands. This girl is impossible, or may be the fairer sex, has it inbuilt, they can't stop from being flirtatious.

I can't hear what they are talking about, but at least, I can say this much that they are twiddling their thumbs 'cause they want to be together.

"Oh, Nikki, you say you love me, and your son is your priority. If that's so, why can't you mend your ways?"

I'm more pissed off with Nikki than I was ever with Presha. She wasn't four-flusher like Nikki. I knew from day one Presha was erratic, and she loved her freedom more than anything else in this world. The time she found she had different interests, she cut loose with me. At least, she wasn't a two-timer.

Dushan pats Nikki on the shoulder and waves at her. She blushes and her eyes glitter.

She finds time to focus back on work. She swings open the door and walks towards me.

'Adie, it's hardly five minutes to twelve o'clock. Let's move to the conference room for a meeting.'

"What a jerk she is? I'm even unable to stand her sight at the juncture. She sucks."

'Ugh! So at last, that idiot has reminded you of the work.

'I don't want you in the room. I can very well manage it without you.

'Oh, crap! I'm sorry if Dushan's going to be there, then I have no right to stop you; otherwise, I don't want to see your face.'

Nikki stifles her tears, 'Adie, it's rude. This is an office; you can't be personal with me.'

'Shut up Nikki! I'm not as versatile as you are. I can't divvy up a female as an assistant in the office and my wife at home. For you, these are two different roles, but for me it's the same lady.'

Nikki's tears are touring her cheeks. Her hands are clasped and she's fidgeting her palms, 'Adie, I'm not your wife.'

'Oh God, it's the way this girl is pressurizing me to marry her.

'No, Nikki; Never; you don't deserve that place. You can't take Presha's place. She was a million times better than you.

'You are a typical whore.'

My phone beeps. It's a call from the conference room. Folks are waiting for me to start the meeting.

Without giving a damn to Nikki, I slam the door and proceed to the meeting room. My brows are cocked, and my jaws are stiff. I hope I don't smack anyone there.

Nikki stands there drowned in an ocean of tears. She's exhausted. She props a hand on the table and sits on a chair in my cabin. She sets her arms folded on the table and face bent on the arms. She's whimpering. She wonders, where is her pleasant surprise?

"Adie's behavior has been obnoxious." She blames her stars for bad luck every time she gets closer to someone. She's sitting there hiding her face. Her mind rambles through various incidents in her life– her marriage, getting closer to me, and my past.

"Oh God! His attitude towards me is in many ways similar to that with Presha. She too might be an innocent girl. Adie seems to have some psychological problem. I need to do something about it. He needs help. Help!" Nikki blinks at her tears and goes back to her chair. She *goggles* for the best psychiatrist in NCR.

'Dr. Bhagat's clinic!'

'Hi, I'm Nikki. I'd like to arrange an appointment to see Dr. Bhagat.'

'When it's convenient for you?'

'Please, I want it as early as it can be, may be, as of today.'

'Ma'am, I'm afraid he can see you only after next Wednesday.'

'It means only after eight days!

'It's urgent.'

'I understand, but nothing I can do about it.'

'Okay, gimme the earliest available time.

'Thursday 26th, at 1:00 p.m.'

'It's okay.'

'Which name should I make an appointment?'

'Nikki'

'Is this the patient name?'

'Nope'

'Can I have your phone no.?'

'98777...........'

'Fine ma'am. You see Dr. Bhagat on the 26th at one o'clock. You'll get a confirmation call from me, one day before due date.'

'Have a good day ma'am.'

'Bye.'

Nikki hangs up the phone. There's isn't a line on her face to reflect any confusion.

"I have a hunch; he needs help."

* * * * *

These official meetings throw me off the balance. A bunch of highbrowed people usually battle out their ego's in wood odor rooms, ironically complicating otherwise simple solutions.

Before this, Nikki has piqued me, and now this meeting is ruffling my feathers. My face moves like a pendulum between the clock on the wall and professionals in the room. I'm waiting, for the clock to strike one o'clock, I can feel my lungs clenching for want of fresh air. Here it goes, the big needle reaches twelve.

'Okay, guys! I feel we aren't going anywhere. We should disperse for the day, and plan to meet again,' I say to the people sitting at the back, as my feet have already positioned me in the doorway.

I know this is rude, but, not beyond the levels the world is being to me.

I push the door of my room and look back at Nikki with a squinted eye. Her face is tilted to the notepad on the table, where she's scribbling something.

I stare at my laptop. Check emails and messenger. Thank God! No one has drowned, as I didn't attend to my emails in the last one hour.

I have an urge to smash something to control my restlessness.

I cock my face towards the glass wall peeping at the maddening traffic outside. It looks so similar to my brain at the moment, several crazy thoughts congesting my mind.

I hear the slight squeak of the door opening.

'Hey, Adie, how was your meeting?' Nikki asks in an unsteady voice.

I don't care to turn my face around, 'I don't want anyone to enter my room till I ask for it.'

I can hear Nikki breathe heavily, 'Sorry,' and she moves out of the room.

I reach back home; I can hear, Nikki is helping out Karan with his homework.

After some time, she comes to my room with a cup of tea.

'Adie, do you mind to munch something with it,' she says, handing over the cup to me.

There's no need to get concerned about me. I thought you weren't coming home today; Why? What happened? Dushan didn't invite you to his home for the night. You slut!'

Nikki yells out of the pain of burning skin.

'You deserve it.' I shove off.

Kabir rushes to my room after hearing a cry of her mother.

The sight of his mother littered with tea, holding her burnt left hand, and groaning in pain; throws Karan into a tizzy. He runs after me with a paperweight in his hand, and as I'm opening the front door to go back to my apartment, he strikes it on my head.

Poor thing misses his target, and it bangs on the door. I lose my temper and smack him.

Karan cries the blues and runs towards Nikki. He's shocked on the new turmoil in his life.

I go back to my apartment; determined, not to look at Nikki again. To put up with her in the office would be a compulsion till one of us makes a shift. I'll do anything to take her out of my sight and mind.

Next day, I'm expecting Nikki to knock at my door. She should apologize for her indecent behavior. I thought last time I explained to her that she should keep herself in check with the opposite sex. This plain and simple thing isn't going to the bottom of her mind.

Neither has she apologized nor has she got bed tea or breakfast for me; she hasn't come at all to see me. She's trying to throw tantrums at me. It's very stereotypical of sleazy females like her.

She isn't there in the office. I see an email in my inbox from Nikki. I feel queasy opening it. Maybe it's her resignation Maybe!

Getting hold of myself, I open it. It says,

It is to inform you that I won't be able to attend the office for a few days due to unavoidable circumstances.

Shit! She must be hunting for a new job. She wants to cut capers with someone else now.

When I reach home, her door is closed.

She hasn't come to office in the last five days. She hasn't even talked to me once in these days. But I know she's inside; I can hear, Karan's voice. I don't understand why? But I want to have a glimpse of her.

Friday morning, I can hear the front door chirr. My heart is pounding fast; it can be no one else but Nikki. At last, I'll see her now. What the hell? The door closes quietly, but there's no one seen or heard.

I scoot down to the lobby. The breakfast is set on the dining table. I know I'm annoyed with her, but still, I want to meet her.

I enter my office floor, and there's a feeling Nikki is somewhere near.

Perhaps, it's the fragrance of her perfume that has prompted me to think so, and there's no esoteric connect between us.

My lips broaden and eyes twinkle. Yeah, I was so right in my assessment! Nikki is here in front of me, her eyes inclined to her laptop and the left hand resting on the working table.

Crap! It completely blew out of my mind; she's hurt, 'cause of my boisterous act that day.

She has a *band-aid* on parts of her hand and blemishes of moist pink skin peeping out of her arm at places.

As I extend my hand to wrench the door of my room, Nikki says, 'Good morning.' There's a silence after that.

I take a second to turn around, 'Good morning, Nikki.' I see Nikki is already working on her laptop. I swivel away my eyes from her and move inside.

The entire day I'm hesitant to flick *101*. I prefer to communicate through emails, and she gives thumbs up to my favored treatment. Not even once she entered my room as if she anyways wanted to get rid of me.

She leaves the office sharp at six o'clock, drop in an email to me that she's off for the day.

I reach back at eight o'clock. As I'm on the last step of the stair, I see Karan entering his apartment. He turns around to close the door, and his eyes fall on me. He's spooky at my site; he rushes inside, leaving the door open. Nikki's not seen around.

As I unlock the front door of my house, I see dinner laid out on the table. What am I? A bloody sucker, a parasite! I'm genuinely remorseful, and I'm desperate to tell it to Nikki.

I immediately order a bouquet of white roses, delivery addressed to Nikki at the office for the next day morning at around nine o'clock with a *Sorry* card.

Nikki is aloof. I see the bouquet placed on her table. She intones 'Good morning,' and in an uncharacteristic insouciance her fingers move to call someone else, without waiting for my response. "Tantrums again! Very quintessential of females!"

I shrug my shoulders and drift inside.

Life is monotonous, till a Saturday morning Nikki comes to me holding a cup of tea in her hand. I scoot over the bed desiring her to sit there. I know it's going to be a binary state, either she's telling me she has found a new job and she's moving out; or even, as her face shows it, she may be out here for a patch up.

She sits on the edge of the bed and after a few minutes silence, 'Adie, yesterday I had gone to meet a psychiatrist.'

'Oh! What happened? I didn't realize I have disturbed you so much.'

'No, Adie, it's not because of you. All this while I have been introspecting and I realized that there's something in my behavior which puts you off. I have never found you prissy with anyone else but me. You are a caring and sensitive man. I respect you for your qualities. I don't want to lose you if something can be changed within me and it saves our relationship; Trust me, I'm prepared to do whatever it might require.'

Nikki sounds so genuine. 'So what did he say?'

'I had an hour long session with him, I shared everything about my life– our relationship and the behavioral concerns you find in me.

'Now he wants to know your perspective, about the situations we were in.'

'It shouldn't be an issue. I can meet him anytime with you.'

'He wants to see you alone.'

'That's fine.'

'When should I fix the appointment with him?'

'As early as possible, if it helps.'

'Maybe Monday afternoon,' Nikki says, trying to put words in my mouth.

'I'm all right, if there's nothing else scheduled for that time,' I'm saying it for the heck of it. I know Nikki is so particular about the nitty gritty of planning.

'I'll call up the clinic to fix it up at two o'clock on Monday.'

'Sounds good.' I wasn't aware, but Nikki had already made an appointment three days before talking it over with me.

Monday, one o'clock: Nikki opens the door, 'Adie, I had confirmed your appointment with Dr. Bhagat for 2:00 p.m. today.

'You'll have to get a move on.'

'Dr. Bhagat???'

'Psychiatrist, I'm consulting,' Nikki rolled her eyes as if the bid she had won is being canceled.

'Oh! Nikki, do I really need to go? I don't want to say anything contemptuous,' I say it with open hands falling apart and squeezed eyes expressing my dilemma.

'Adie, you won't be disrespectful to me at all. Rather, you are extending a favor. Say your real feelings. That's it.'

I stand there with my hand covering the mouth. I look at Nikki, and desperation in her eyes to hear a *yes* from me.

'Okay. Text me his address. I'll leave in another five minutes.'

I can see a slight smile tweaking Nikki's mouth. She moves her fingers a few times on her phone, and I hear a beep on my cell.

Oh God! I can't believe it, but I'm there in the clinic of a Psychiatrist. But it's altogether for a different purpose. I want to help Nikki, she's a great female and on top of everything she runs my life nowadays.

Dr. Bhagat calls me inside. It's a big hall colored in beige and teak wood furniture ensemble the place. There's a couch and a coffee table in the left corner of the entry door. The right end has a brown chaise lounge, one white fabric recliner, and a side table.

Doc's not around. I sit on the couch and start flipping through the pages of *The Times of India* strewn on the coffee table.

Betrayed husband kills his wife; the headline punches my heart. Beside me, I see a door open, and Dr. Bhagat makes an entry into the room.

He extends his hand towards me, 'Hi, I'm Sumer Bhagat. You are Aadir, right.'

'Yep. You can call me Adie.

'Oh! Hi.'

He looks at what I was reading with a squinted eye and remarks, 'Crap! These dailies nowadays are full of outrageous stories like the one you were reading just now.'

'No Doc, I feel they all make sense as they are a reflection of our society. Immorality in our society is creeping like a termite; especially, present-time females have no ethics left to carry home.'

'Adie, I feel you are biased for females. Men are equally responsible for increased levels of peccancy.'

'Do you mind if I call you Sumer?'

'Please go ahead.'

'Sumer, men, had always been like that, it's the new breed of females that's being promiscuous.'

'It can have another facet. They are more educated now and are getting liberated, which they deserved to have been a long back; maybe they are squirting now.'

'Doc, I have always abhorred the idea of giving undue concession to women 'cause of their legacy.'

'Uh-huh…

'You don't like freedom. Do you?' Sumer smirks.

'I'm a freedom freak; I'll not hear of anyone dictating me.'

'But you like to swivel women,' Doc quipped.

'I hope you're treating Nikki, and not hiding a multitude of sins with her in the wrap of my attitude,' I grinned.

'Not at all!

'She's seeking my help and I have to extend it earnestly, that's my job. But Adie, these are sensitive issues. You are the one to bring it to the fore, so I need to understand you better before analyzing her,' Sumer says it with broadened eyes and stretched face.

'I understand Doc. I'm all out to help her,' I say, exhaling the initial pique.

'Fantastic!

'Adie, tell me everything about you. The straighter from the shoulder you'll be that much fruitful it's going to be for all of us,' Doc says with firmness in his voice.

'I'm sure you aren't a micro expression reader. They are a pain in the butt.'

'I'm not. But I think there's a story behind it. Ha ha...' Sumer steals his eyes as if he isn't interested in dragging this discussion.

'Hhhhhh.'

'Okay, let's start,' Doc says, getting down to the business.

'I'm Aadir Chopra, Director... Nikki is like a friend. My life is stalled if she isn't around. I like her, but she says she loves me. I haven't observed anything sleazy in her behavior with the males till I moved in to stay with her; otherwise, I would have evaded her,' and as I'm reciting my life to him, there's a pause....

'Are you tired, Adie?'

'No Doc, it's about my ex-wife. I'm not sure if I need to tell you that.'

'Oh yes! You need to confide everything in me, Adie. Let's keep it for our next meeting.'

'Do we need to have one? I thought I've shared enough about me with you.'

'But I'll like to know more. Till now, I have only judged you as a sensitive and a possessive man. I need to find out more to analyze how much your attitude has impacted your assessment about Nikki.'

'You mean it's my problem.'

'I'm not saying it, but I feel she has a right to the fair diagnosis.'

'Sure.'

'What about Friday for our next appointment?'

'It's fine. I'll ask Nikki to confirm it.'

'Good day.'

'You too.'

It's five o'clock. I decide to go back home. Nikki won't be back by this time, and I know Karan won't be inclined to spend time with me. Now he's afraid of me.

I'm tired, the meeting was stressful in parts. Maybe, a glass of red wine and music can help soothe my brain.

I hear the footsteps of Nikki. She's got the dinner for me. She let out a long sigh outside my room.

'Please come in Nikki.'

'Hey, Adie, how was your meeting with Dr. Bhagat?'

'I hope it's helpful.'

'I can't be more thankful to you,' she touches my hand, and then withdraws it quickly as if a spark has struck her. She cast down her eyes in shame.

I hold her arms, 'It's not your fault. At least, you have come forward to accept it. I'm sure everything will be fine.'

'Yep,' she says, calmly.

'Nikki, can we have dinner together?'

'I'll have to ask Karan if he's ok.'

'Can I help you?'

Nikki nods and moves to her apartment. I follow her.

Chapter 10

'Karan, I'm sorry. I promise this won't happen again,' and I hug him. I can feel my shirt wet on the torso.

'Baby, don't cry. Don't cry. It's okayyy. Let's go out for dinner. *McDonald's*!!! Yeah, right.'

Karan smiles, the smile spread across his face.

It's difficult to control my nerves when I look at Nikki. I realize she's sick. My mind can understand it, but there's no way I can explain it to my heart. I have decided not to go out with her till she get's treated, so I take out Karan with me to *McDonald*. I know Nikki understands it.

* * * * *

Friday afternoon: I'm sitting with Dr. Bhagat.

'So, did you ask Presha why Yuvi was there in your home?'

'What was to be asked? She was a whore. She betrayed me,' I say with stoned eyes and clenched hands. My forehead is covered with sprinkles of water. I want to call out at the top of my voice, blow out the pain of incisions on my faith.

'Did you try to stop her?'

'Yes, I did, but there was no point, she never wanted a fixed abode. She had made up her mind to discard me,' and I burst into tears.

Sumer hands me a glass of water. I take a tissue from the side table and wipe off my face. I look at him with zipped lips and a broad smile. His eyes were silently exploring every expression of mine.

'Adie, if it's too stuffy we can plan to meet some other time.'

'No Doc, let's do it today. I don't want to live those moments again.'

'Adie, anything else you'll like to tell me.'

'I think I have laid down everything.'

'BTW, did you ever visit a psychiatrist after anxiety attack in Singapore.'

'Never. I know I'm perfectly okay.'

'Uh-huh…!' Doc's hand is covering his chin as if he's in deep thoughts.

'Sumer, any worries!'

'Adie, I need to share something with you, though, a few tests need to be performed before I can be sure about it, but,' Sumer looks into my eyes as if his brain is still processing the words.

'But???'

'My assessment of your symptoms, and hearing about your marital experience suggests that you might be suffering from *Delusion of infidelity*, it's a psychotic illness.'

'Are you suggesting me that I'm mad?'

'No Adie, we are trying to diagnose your problem.'

'I thought I'm here to help out Nikki, but this has turned out to be different. Oh! Ha!'

'Adie, you have an issue with your partner, and your partner came to me for consultation. I couldn't have assessed her before talking to you. Now it looks, there might also be a problem with you as well.'

'Doc, I'm perfectly okay. I have never faced any failure in life, and I have always lived my life on my own terms. And now you tell me, Aadir Chopra, who used to be an ideal for many people, is mentally sick. Holy Crap! I can't take it.'

'Adie, first and foremost, I'm not concluding anything yet, I just expressed to you my apprehension.'

'Doc, I fail to understand what made you think so?'

'Your symptoms.'

'Like…'

'Accusing partner of looking or giving attention to other males, lack of trust, controlling the partner's social behavior, threatening to harm others and several others.

'I know Adie it'll be impossible for me to convince you of your problem, ironically, this is again one of the symptoms.

'Adie, to the greatest extent you need to trust me. Still, there are a few tests to confirm our diagnosis. In case they are positive, believe me, this can be treated–some therapies and medication.

'What about Nikki?'

'I need to have a few more sessions with her, maybe one with two of you together.

'Adie, let me say one thing–you are very fortunate to have Nikki in your life. She's ready to do anything for you. Such people are jewels; you don't find them so easily in life.'

'I know she's a gem of a female.'

I'm perplexed. This is coming to me as a shock. I'm cocksure there's no problem with me. Why the doctor can't see how right I was about Presha? Then, how can my assessment about Nikki be wrong? But if Nikki needs my help, I'm ready to take his crap.

'Okay, Doc, which tests need to be done?'

'*Blood test dopamine levels and Thyroid Hormonal Assay.*

'Adie, I find you are moderately depressed too. I'll start you on a mild antidepressant, *fluoxetine*. I'm sure whether you suffer from delusion or not, you'll feel better.

'Great! See you after two months.'

'Bye.'

Nikki isn't sharing it with me, but she's in constant touch with Dr. Sumer.

Doc may be calling her intentionally so frequently, he must be nearing sixty and at this age, men are usually overtly attracted by younger females.

I don't know where is this going? In the disguise of treatment, he may exploit Nikki. Anyways, at this age too, he's handsome; he's established and filthy rich. What else, a female needs?

It's afternoon, Nikki is not there in the office. She hasn't informed me of her whereabouts, just email,

Due to some personal work, I'm leaving early.

* * * * *

'Nikki, I shouldn't forget to mention it, you need to be careful with Adie. He can be violent any time, you can't prejudge what can trigger that reaction. If it happens anytime, don't argue or convince him about the facts, just, bound out the place and call me.'

'Can it get so bad, Doc?'

'Nikki, still we have no confirmation about his ailment. I'm just warning you of what can happen.'

'Okay,' Nikki wipes her face.

'Nikki, we need to find out something more about his ex-wife. What Adie has narrated will create a suspicion in any one's mind. And above all, Presha's lifestyle and passion for freedom can confuse anyone.

'We need to hear from her before any conclusion can be drawn. Till then, I can't put him on any antipsychotic medicine. Yes, I can plan a therapeutic session with him, but that, too, I'll have a ground to do so only after the test results.

There's a beep on the Doc's phone. The voice says something, and Sumer's nose and forehead scrunch up.

'Nikki, things are complicated. Adie's, test results are clear. I have no basis to convince him for any treatment, and, in fact, he doesn't even need one. We don't have any clinical evidence of the disease. It could be just a resentful ingrained belief against females.'

'Doc, we must not forget that he felt it the first time only after his first marriage. If it's only bias, then why he hasn't expressed it anytime for his girlfriends, sister or even for that matter his mother.

'Nikki, I'm not saying that I can't identify a problem, but there has to be either a strong pathological or clinical evidence to support it.'

'I'll try to get in touch with Presha, and if possible, make her talk to you.'

'Nikki, it'll be great.

'But remember, medicines aren't as useful in this problem, as your handling of him. Don't ever make him realize that he has any mental illness. Your emotional support and appropriate approach can be the best treatment.'

'Okay, Doc, thanks.'

'Bye Nikki.'

'Bye.'

Nikki is a tough girl. Life hasn't drawn to a close from challenging her to unfold her pleasant surprise bundle; she's determined to open it one day. She's having cognitive sessions with Sumer, and she's equally concerned about me. It's only 'cause of her, I take anti- depressants; otherwise, I know I'm perfectly fine.

* * * * *

The phone is ringing, but no one is picking it up. At last, 'Ms. Chopra!'

'Hello aunty, this is Nikki.'

'How are you, Nikki? How's Adie? Long time, you haven't visited me.'

'Aunty, there's something I need to discuss with you. Can I see you today?'

'Yeah, of course; you can come anytime.'

'I'll be there at around four o'clock.'

Nikki puts down the phone. She shakes the pen in her hand and taps it on her lips.

She drops an email to me and leaves early from the office. I peep at her; she's packing her things to leave for somewhere, but where? I don't ask her, I'm waiting for her to say it to me. She walks away, and I sit there with folded hands.

Chapter 11

'Namaste.'

'Namaste; Please come in, Nikki.

Nikki sits in the living room. Nikki is stealing her eyes from Muma as if she's buying time to collect her thoughts. It's not easy for anyone to tell a mother that her son, perhaps, is a psycho.

Muma sees her enigma, but she thinks Nikki is there to talk about our marriage with her. She smiles.

'What would you like to drink, Nikki?'

'Aunty, I'll have tea.'

Muma gets the tea and sets the serving tray on the center table.

Handing over a cup to Nikki, she says, 'You mentioned you need my help for something. What's it?'

'Aunty, I want to know about Presha.'

'Presha!!! I thought you loved Adie, and that's why you both are together. Now, why do you want information about Presha.'

'I want to understand her better. Adie never talks about Presha, but somehow I feel he still loves her.'

'Nikki, I don't think, they were made for each other. I even don't know what actually happened between them, but I can say this much– girls like Presha can't live this institution for long; they value their freedom above everything else and marriage involves sacrifices.'

Nikki gazes at my mother, and her mind ponders on Muma's thoughts. "*No mother can wait to find fault in her son's spouse, and if she's ex, she's the biggest blunder in this world.*"

'Aunty, you are right. But I want to start my life on a firm footing. Dwindling minds don't lead us anywhere. If Adie wants to explore his mind again, he has every right to do it.'

'It's okay if you feel so. What help do you want from me? I can't tell you about Presha as I hardly knew her.'

'I think, Charlie can be of some help.'

'It will be nice if you can share his contact details with me.'

'I can give you his mobile.'

'Please.

'Aunty, may I request you, not to tell Adie about it. I know him, he'll be hurt.'

'Uh….'

Nikki is at home before me.

'Today, you left early. Is everything okay?' I say, trying not to sound too inquisitive.

'Yeah, Sumer…'

Before she can complete, I say, 'I called up Sumer but he didn't tell me you were there.'

'No, Sumer asked me to get some tests done. I wasn't with him.'

'Oh! Okay.'

Medicines seem to be doing their magic. I don't lose my temper so quickly, even if I know the woman in front of me is making a fool of me. Let's see how long the voodoo works.

I'm staying in with Nikki; though, I feel she's a little withdrawn from me. Maybe she's pretending so, as not to give Karan a sense of isolation, he still isn't comfortable with me.

Nikki's with Karan. Its lull in her room; it seems, Karan has gone off to sleep. Nikki has placed a *fluoxetine* tablet and a glass of water on the night table. After taking the medicine, I switch off the light. I have closed my eyes, but I know, Nikki is awake, as beams of yellow light from her room are peeping in through the gaps round the door. I wish I can talk to her.

Oh! I can hear her speak in hushed tones. I never knew anti- depressants can inebriate someone. I'm suffering from hallucinations.

I calm the nerves, and try to decant my mind.

No, still I can hear her voice. She's speaking to someone, may be, over the phone or is there someone in her room. I can only hear Nikki, I think she's over the phone.

I keep an ear to the ground to find whom she's talking to.
'Charlie!'

'Hello Charlie, I'm Nikki; Adie's PA.'

'Oh! How can I help you?' Charlie says, curtly.

'Charlie, I want to know about Presha. Can you give me her contact details?'

'Why the hell in this world you want her details?' Charlie sounds worried. An amicable person like Charlie can't be rude to anyone, he must be anxious.

'I need it to help Adie. He's in trouble.'

'Sorry, I don't remember what your name is, but please leave her alone. She already has had a lot of trouble 'cause of him. I told him they were not made for each other, but Adie always has his own way.'

'I know that, but, I also know he loves her enormously.'

'It's bullshit! Do you know what happened between them?'

'No, I don't. I want to meet Presha to know it, and also to tell her how much he loves her.'

'You know, how barbarous, he was with her; can someone be so cruel to his love?

'I think he never loved her, it was just his passion for the challenges he was attracted to her. And it became difficult for him to accept his defeat when he couldn't tame Presha.

'I know my sister, she can be anything but not a floozy,' Charlie says in a cracked voice. Nikki can't see him; but she can feel the tears rolling down his cheeks.

'Sorry! Charlie; my intent never was, to hurt you. I want to help Adie, he's mentally ill.'

Anyways, I'm unable to hear what she's saying, but now I can't even hear her whisper. What! I can again hear her voice.

'Charlie, are you there?'

'Yes, what did you say just now?'

'I'm not sure, but he's suffering from delusion. I feel, Presha can only sway him for treatment.'

'How?'

'I have a hunch that she's true.

'If somehow, I can prove it to Adie that he judged her wrong, he might agree to his treatment,' Nikki says in a vibrant voice.

'I don't know what you can do; but, if the fact, that she's fighting for her life 'cause of him can evince her sincerity, then you can tell him.'

'What?'

Now I can hear Nikki. It looks as if she's planning, some conspiracy; and the person on the other side laid a condition which has baffled her.

'What's the matter?' Nikki sounds anxious!

'She's suffering from cirrhosis, last stage. Presha decided to die than to live without Adie. She drowned herself in alcohol to flee from Adie's thoughts badgering her mind; though, she knew it was poison for her.'

'Why did no one stop her?'

'We weren't aware of it until last month when I visited Singapore to meet my fiancée, I found her in ICU. It's too late now,' Charlie whimpers. He can't believe that he's talking about his Lil sister who has never cared to stop for anything, but the man whom she loved the most in this world made her helpless.

'Where's she now?'

'She's in Singapore; she has refused to come back to India.'

'Charlie, I'm so sorry for her. All the more it's urgent I should meet her. To tell her– how much Adie loves her; but he's unaware that destiny has played fowl with him.

'Presha rhymes in his heart; he thinks she has left him in a lurch. Her infidelity is just a delusion of his mind, and the irony is, he doesn't have any control over it. Maybe, if they know the truth even now, a few things can be repaired if they can't be undone.'

'I'm not sure, but please! For God sake! Let her die in peace– the way she's always lived, on her own terms.'

'Charlie, don't even say these words. Adie will also not live without her.'

'I know, I have lost the two precious people in my life.'

'Please! Let's not surrender to destiny so easily. I'm hopeful, pleasant surprises will unfold.'

Again, there's silence. I think she has hung up the phone. Can it be a new suitor or is she going back to her husband? Whatever, she should be candid with me. I don't think any therapy can change this whore.

I'm restless. I want to butcher her, the way she's doing to my faith. I gulp a sleeping pill and get off to sleep.

When I wake up in the morning, I'm a bit relaxed. It's not that I don't remember last night, but I know Nikki is mentally ill. I need to talk to Sumer. Nikki shouldn't land up in the wrong hands.

Sumer hears me out, and he calls me to his clinic.

'Adie, Nikki was here before you. She's disturbed. Her husband is harassing her; you need to understand and support her.'

'Doc, she was on the phone for almost an hour with him. She could have disconnected the phone or called me; I would have given that swine, good piece of my mind.

'She didn't do either of it; and on top of everything she posed her ignorance in the morning. I waited for her to say something, and she completely ignored me.'

'Adie, there's nothing like that. She loves you; it's just that she's finding it difficult to get rid of her husband.'

'Doc, you may be, but I'm not convinced. She's been fooling us.'

'Adie, I know for sure she's not lying. If I don't trust my patients, I can never treat them.

'You need to believe unless you are proven wrong, and above all, you can't compel anyone to be loyal to you. If she doesn't want a relationship with you, so be it.'

'Trust! Uh!'..............

Doc talks to me for more than an hour, and I don't even realize that I'm having a session with him.

Anyways, I'm feeling relaxed. He has given me some more medicines to manage the stress Nikki causes me. I take a deep breath and bound out of the Doc's clinic.

I reach back home. Nikki is avoiding an eye contact with me, she's hiding something. Oh God! Only an idiot can believe her.

In the morning, I see a handwritten note by Nikki on my night table,

It's critical. I need to go out for two days. Karan is going along with me. Sorry, I can't write more than this.

Bullshit! I told the Doc that she was double crossing. I call up Sumer and tell him about her note. His treatment has miserably failed, and I don't have any depression. I'm perfectly fine, but this world is bent upon in turning me into a psycho.

This time, I'm rude with Sumer; and he has lost his credibility. Doctors have a noble profession; they should serve in the best interest of humanity. On the contrary, they misguide their patients just for money. It's sickening.

Chapter 12

A reminder pops up on my screen.

Oh! I should be at *Hyatt* for an investor conference; my feet, sway slightly; how could Nikki forget to remind me of such an important event in the morning?

Uh! I put down the cradle, clenching my lips. She's not there.

I rush to *Hyatt*, and I'm here in the hall before the start of the opening speech. As usual, the conference is boring; a bunch of enthusiasts promising a sponsored journey to the moon in the next couple of months. And I bet they'll never shell out a penny on any odyssey, citing poor visibility of the moon as an excuse.

I move out for a tea break.

No, she can't be here! I clean my eyes and again look at the corner table in the lobby. It's Rachel; she has a flirtatious smile on her face, and she's gazing at an old man in front of her. The man seems to be a bastard with lust in his eyes, ready to pounce on her.

My blood is running in a marathon. I have a clenched fist clobbering into the palm of the other hand. I want to whack Rachel and the man.

I call her. She's unfazed, her phone doesn't buzz. Maybe, it's switched off.

Cheap woman, I text her. I know, she isn't looking at my message, but I don't know how to overcome the embarrassment she's causing me.

I go into the hall, a new speaker is presenting. I sit there, trying to focus on what he's explaining. After every second my eyes drop on the phone lying on the round table in front of me. Rachel hasn't replied back. My mind is on pins and needles, and I'm drenched in sweat on a wintry day.

Finally, I move out to look for her. No one is seen on the corner table. I look around to see if they have shifted to some other place. I text, again.

A bitch can't be my sister.

I can't sit in the conference room anymore. I call Sumer to arrange an urgent appointment with him. At last, he has succeeded in tying me to his apron.

I'm still restless. My eyes can't stop looking at the phone. Rachel isn't replying back. She'll never wait so long to hit me back. She's still with the asshole. I was always so right about her; she's going to bring shame to our family.

I text, again.

Relationship ends.

Now, I immediately hear a beep.

Do you know what a brother stands for? You psycho, get yourself treated.

She's a shameless woman. When I have caught her red-handed, she's accusing me of being a lunatic.

* * * * *

I'm at Doc's clinic lying on his chaise lounge. I'm so tired, I need to relax.

Nikki is no more a part of our discussion. Today, it's Rachel. Two of us look shocked. Perhaps, I'm stunned at Rachel's immorality, and Doc at his assessment. I have proved him wrong at every place. I'm not boasting of my accomplishment, but I'm distressed at the outcome.

Sumer advises me to continue with the medicines as I need to maintain calm in such tough times.

When I arrive at my apartment, I hear some noises from Nikki's home. It looks, she's back.

I'm already perturbed. I don't want to meet her now. I feel like killing her at the point. I go home, pour a glass of red wine and lay in the bed; every sip takes me down the memory lane of my life. I feel so lonely and worry sick.

Nikki calls me for dinner. Her voice is as vibrant as it can be. She doesn't seem to have an idea about my feelings for her. I refuse to join her, and she tells me that she'll get me something to eat after Karan gets off to sleep. I'm sure she wants to break some news to me.

She comes with a tray and sets it on the dining table. I'm starving, so without getting into any mess with her, I start eating the food. She sits on a chair on the other side of the table.

When I'm almost done, 'Adie, you didn't ask about my whereabouts for the last three days?'

'Nikki, don't start it. I'm really not interested to know where you were. Moreover, you aren't forced to stay with me. In fact, none is.

'But if I want to tell you.'

'No point. I know you'll never tell the truth.'

'If I had the choice not to say it to you, then, trust me, I would have never told you the truth. But now it's not for you, it's for Presha's life.'

'What the hell you have to do with Presha,' I flinch from the chair.

'Adie, Presha is struggling for her life. After you left, she became dipsomaniac; she hasn't stopped drinking even after she was diagnosed with cirrhosis.

'Cirrhosis, fourth stage.'

'Damn it! I'm not to be blamed. She was always a bloody drunkard.

'Why don't you give the credit to his sweetheart, Mike,' I'm annoyed, but why am I missing my pulse?

'No. It's only 'cause of you, she's here today. She loves you, and doesn't want a life without you.'

'Why? What happened to her Mike and Yuvi.'

'They are there, supporting her life as best buddies. But none is her love.'

'Nikki, you aren't good at making stories,' I smash the plate on the floor.

'Please Adie, for God sake, listen to me and for once trust me. I was in Singapore for the last three days. When I reached there, Presha was in ICU; and Mike and Yuvi were there with her in the hospital. Though, it wasn't the right time, but I spoke to them about Presha. They told me that she's crazy about you, and perhaps, your misunderstanding started when you found Yuvi in your house in the morning.'

'I repent, why did I leave the bastard? I should have killed him there and then.'

'Presha called him there.'

'No wonder! She's a slut.'

'It was her first symptom of Cirrhosis: she had felt a severe pain in her stomach, and she had none to call. You were traveling, so she called Yuvi in urgency. By the time Yuvi reached, the pain was subsiding and they thought it was some gastric attack. It went unattended. After it, you know it better– what had happened. You never gave her a chance to say anything; and she didn't fight to tell you something. She was brutally hit.

'Adie, please meet her once. Maybe, something can still be done to save her life.'

I can feel the goosebumps. I want to scream, but above all, I don't want to believe Nikki.

'Why did you go there?' I scream at Nikki.

'Dr. Sumer wanted to know about Presha. He feels you are suffering from the *delusion of infidelity*.'

'No, I'm not a psycho. It's only by chance that it has happened to Presha. I'm not the reason. She could have told me on several occasions.

'But I'll definitely go and meet her. Not 'cause you or someone else is telling me to do that. I'm going as I still love her and will always do so.'

There's radiance on Nikki's face. She's a funny girl! She says she loves me; and I'm telling her I love Presha, and she's ecstatic about it. Reading a female's mind is difficult.

* * * * *

'Nikki, I need to meet Adie's Mom,' Sumer looks at Nikki with inquisitive eyes, and a blank face.

'Is there any problem Doc? I hope Adie should be okay after meeting Presha.'

'I hope so. Nikki, do you have any idea about Adie's relationship with his sister.'

'He hardly speaks about her.'

'Have you ever met her, or seen her?'

'I saw her picture at Adie's house.'

'How does she look?'

'She's gorgeous.'

'Ah ha! Even I anticipated so.

'Nikki, it seems Adie is also suffering from sibling jealousy. The case is getting difficult day by day.'

'When is Adie going to Singapore?'

'This weekend.'

'Please ensure you also go along with him, and fix my appointment with his mother before you leave.'

'Doc, can't he go alone? It'll be difficult for both of us to be away from the office at the same time.'

'You need to go, Nikki,' Sumer was emphatic.

'Okay, Doc.'

'Bye, Nikki.'

Chapter 13

Nikki and Karan tag along with me to Singapore.

I can feel butterflies in my stomach. I'm meeting Presha after almost a year, except a glimpse of her I had at the court.

Presha is still staying with Mike. The thought of seeing her at his house is scrunching my heart, and stressing my nerves. I wish Nikki would have been with me at the moment.

I enter Mike's apartment.

'Booooooooom!!! I smash to smithereens. I can't exhale. I'm trying hard; breath is not leaving my chest. But, I'm not dead.

"This thing called love I just cann't handle it

"this thing called love I must get round to it

"I ain't ready

"Crazy little thing called love......,"

The song is echoing in my ears. And my eyes aren't yet stoned, I can see tresses falling on Presha's face, her dark big bold eyes are still dancing, and a crescent moon in her nose is still shining. Presha looks so beautiful.

'How are you, Adie?' a faint voice asks me, and she tries to lift herself up on the bed.

I dash towards her and hold her in my hands. My eyes are entangled with her. But her eyes are yellow, propped against dark patches; her skin is yellowish-red as a rising sun; her lips are two blue serpentine lines; her eyes can barely open themselves, and her hair is tied back in a tiny knot. She can't be Presha.

Yes, she's Presha. Tears aren't stopping to slide from my eyes. How can God be so cruel? Why did she meet me?

She tries to open her eyes.

'Stop crying Adie, you have drenched my shirt.'

'Presha, you should have called me,' I cover my face with both the hands and let my body slide down the bed until I squat on the floor.

Presha holds my hands and wipes off my cheeks, 'Adie, I'm ready to die a hundred deaths with memories of your nonpareil love, but can't live to see hatred for me in your eyes.'

'Presha, they were small issues; we could have solved them. I only wanted you to be loyal to me.'

'I was, and will always be.'

'No, Presha. You were charmed by Mike. Still, you are with him.

'Okay, we can always argue once you get well,' I say putting a hand on Presha's cheek.

'Where's Nikki?' Presha asks with wandering eyes. I flush, I don't know why?

'Nikki is checking out an apartment for us.'

'What do you mean?' Presha looks anxious as if the thought of moving away from Mike has sent her jitters.

'We can't stay here with Mike; we need to have a place of our own. I'll stay with you till you are okay,' I say smiling at Presha. My heart aches at her innocence, but my mind refuses to accept her purity. Her illness is the punishment for the deeds which she shouldn't have done. I'm clear in my consciousness, I'm here since I love her, and not 'cause of any guilt.

'I love you, Adie.'

I'm quiet, as I don't want to accept something which I'm not convinced of.

We shift to our apartment. Nikki goes back to India as she has the job to attend, and Karan can't be off from school for long. To my surprise, neither Yuvi nor Mike appeared in our new house to meet Presha. However, a day later, Presha's mother arrives to take care of her.

She almost faints looking at Presha. On seeing, her once an ebullient daughter, lying in a groggy and dormant state, she's shocked. She wraps Presha in her arms, and cries relentlessly; till Presha musters energy from somewhere, and shrieks at her, 'Ma, I'm still alive.'

The hue and cry of Mom and daughter settle after some time. Ma proves to be a significant support as Presha is feeble and handicapped. She needs assistance in almost every work. I wonder how Mike was doing it single- handedly.

Ma was unaware of her illness, I'm not sure if Charlie was aware of it. I haven't spoken to him for ages now.

Ma tells me that my friend Nikki called her up, and Charlie immediately arranged for her bookings. Maybe, Charlie is too annoyed with me, that's why, he has avoided accompanying Ma; he doesn't want to see me. Nikki is smart enough to anticipate everything; she was aware that alone, I won't be able to handle Presha.

* * * * *

'Nikki, can we meet today,' Dr. Sumer calls Nikki.

'Yeah, Doc; at what time should I come? If convenient, please fix it in the afternoon.'

'Okay, come at two o'clock.'

'Fine Doc, I'll be there.'

Nikki is sitting with Sumer, and he looks a little perplexed.

'Nikki, as you know, I met Adie's Mom a few days back; she narrated a few incidents which have baffled me about his problem.'

'Doc, what is it now?'

'Nikki, last time when you were in Singapore, Adie came to me. He was accusing his sister of bad character, based on some incident which happened in the hotel that day. I gave him an ear, but it had further raised my concerns about his mental illness.

'I wanted to meet his mother to analyze if he's suffering from sibling jealousy. But, now I think it's something much deeper and complicated than that,' Nikki looks at the Doc with widened eyes, her hands clasped together.

'His mother told me, he had been ultra protective about his sister, Rachel; once he had smacked a three-year-old boy when he was himself seven, as the boy had kissed Rachel on her birthday,' Nikki listens dumbfounded.

'Since her birth, he has never liked any male interacting with her, and whenever he found her even talking to an outsider, he went berserk. The family has never given any special heed to it, as they considered it as his inherent nature; though, Adie's mother agreed that his behavior had caused a lot of stress to Rachel.'

'Funny!' Nikki says for the heck of it.

'No, it's not funny. This is an indication that his problem might be deeply rooted.'

'Doc, it could be just over possessiveness for his sister,' Nikki says with conviction, shunning off Sumer's concerns.

'But it's unusual. How many kids of age seven you know get conscious about protecting their siblings from the opposite sex?'

'Maybe, none,' Nikki frowns.

'Yeah! You are right, it's unusual. And any unusual patterns of behavior, emotion and thought are called abnormality.'

'So?'

'So, there's some abnormality about him, which has gone unattended, and now it has surfaced in an additional form, it's manifesting itself as *delusion of infidelity*.'

'What can it mean?' Nikki says sticking out her hands.

'It could be some old scars on his soul!' Sumer looks astounded.

'What? Are you referring to his previous birth? That sounds like a tale. I'm not sure if I even believe in reincarnation. Do you?'

'Though, reincarnation is viewed with heavy skepticism as it lacks scientific proof, yet a lot of research is being done all over the world on the subject. Various cases are being cited by the people who have been treated by past birth regression.

'Nikki, this is first of its kind in my life history, but I think it's worth trying on those lines. If you want, you can go for a second opinion. Anyways, I'm not an expert to perform it; we'll have to consult some past life therapist.'

'Doc, you know his case the best; so I'll request you to decide whatever needs to be done. I have full faith in you, and so do I feel Adie should have. If you find past life regression is the option, let's plan accordingly.

'I know it'll be difficult for us to convince Adie, but then pleasant surprises don't unfold till you take up challenges,' Nikki grins with confidence.

* * * * *

23rd Feb 2011: After fifteen days, I receive a call from Nikki, though, she has been calling in between to inquire about Presha's welfare, but this time it's for me. She tells me that I'm required in the office, so I need to go back. Maybe, once I'm there, I can ask for a transfer to our Singapore office.

Presha hasn't even started recovering, and I need to leave her for a few days. It's a struggle for me to keep her away from drinking. Her body demands it now. She's got so addicted to alcohol, her body revolts if she doesn't get it; but, if I give her what she craves for, then she's moving closer to her end with a tremendous speed.

I'm cursing myself for abandoning her in the first place. I always knew she's reckless, and can do anything for her perversity. But, I always loved her; I could have been more patient, even if she wanted to run out on me. I can't let her go. Life can't mean anything to me without her.

I call up my doctor friend to keep a check on her, though, she's under the supervision of a dedicated team of physicians. In case of emergency, I know without saying, Yuvi and Mike are omnipresent.

Ma is there to take care of her; but I'm not sure how much she can control her spoilt brat. I think Ma wouldn't have contributed much in making her what she's today. Some kids are, by birth, blessed to be a pain in the neck for their parents, she's one of them.

27th Feb 2011, Sunday: I'm in Delhi. I have missed Karan, all these days. He's a great kid. Till the day, I reproach myself for torturing him, though, it was totally unintentional. I feel embarrassed to stay at Nikki's apartment, I move on to my own after saying *Hi* to her.

Nikki calls me for lunch. She tells me about Sumer's opinion. But I don't think there's any problem with me. And what's more, talking about past birth is so primitive. I rebuff the thought and even refuse to visit Dr. Sumer in future.

'Nikki, I had gone to the doc for you, to help in your treatment. I know I don't have any problem. Maybe, it was situational.'

'And, maybe if not. Adie, don't you dream of a stress-free life with Presha, when everything was pristine. Dr. Sumer is a competent psychiatrist; and if, he has suggested something, at least, you should consider it once.'

'Okay! If you insist!'

'Right now, I don't have the time. I'll go to the office tomorrow, and apply for transfer to Singapore. Meanwhile, I'll operate from home there. But I promise I'll definitely think over your proposal once Presha's fine.'

Nikki's face clenches, and she's sulking. It's clear that I'm going away from her. But she's the one to plan it. *It seems, no matter how stupendous a human being you are, there's always an evil in you, and it counters the good whenever your own interests are harmed. It's natural.*

'I hope you'll come back with Presha next time, and complete your treatment.'

'I have my fingers crossed,' and I leave her place to go to my parent's house.

Muma is exhilarated to see me; she hugs me with a force as if she has found her lost son. Papa is not left behind; he too embraces me, though, with a minor exertion but non-partisan warmth.

Muma tells me that she met Dr. Sumer when I was away. Poor Nikki! She's so considerate of me. I wish I can reciprocate her someday. Neither Muma shares the details of her meeting with Sumer with me, nor do I broach the subject further.

I can feel she's worried about my illness, which never existed; and also about my personal life, which like any other parent, she acquiesces to GOD.

I stay for a night with my parents, as I'll be off to Singapore within a few days. I'm clueless when I'll see them again.

I anticipated that I'll be in India for a week, but it has been more than two weeks I'm still here; I'll be transferred to Singapore office in due course, but for now I'll work for the Indian Division from Singapore office or home there.

I bid adieu to Nikki and Karan. Karan clings around my neck; and I hand over to him his dream, an Xbox.

I hug Nikki; I can feel the vibrations in her body, thud of her broken heart. But the beauty of Nikki is she endeavors to tell me good-bye with a beam on her face.

Chapter 14

I'm back in my old world; old seems like gold.

Presha's eyes glitter on seeing me, they look like diamonds studded in gold. She's still yellow, no visible signs of improvement in her health. Though, doctors tell me that control over her alcohol intake and rejuvenated spirit will surely help her recover, but liver transplant is the primary treatment, and we should start hunting for a donor.

I can be a living donor. My blood group is the same as of Presha, *B+*; that's the prerequisite to be a donor. After performing certain tests and doing some evaluation like *Chest X-ray, ECG*, and *abdominal ultrasound*, they'll confirm if I can save her life. I know I'm perfectly fine, a healthy donor. Charlie can be a fallback; he's willing to donate a portion of the liver for his loving sister. He's also B+. I'm sure everything will be okay.

I'm sitting with Presha caressing her hand, which is the remains of entangled muscles now; while she's lying on the bed, watching TV.

'Adie, can I switch off the TV? I want to talk to you.'

'Yes, Nightingale, anything for you?'

'The name sounds like music to my ears,' Presha says with a mystical face.

A cold shiver runs through my spine, what she's going to unravel?

'Oh! Presha, I'll always love you,' I clasp her with both the hands as if I'm guilty of going away from her.

'What? If something happens to me,' her eyes are piercing my face, my entire body to convey me something.

'I'll not exist after that,' I say, sealing her lips with my hand.

'Adie, you're a hard-headed man; it's a fact that life never stops for anyone. It goes on....,' Presha's lips are as dry as wood. She exerts to speak.

'Hold on! Don't talk!' I hand over a glass of water to her; she swigs it.

'I need to know,' Presha looks at me with anxious eyes.

'I'll live, and wait for this heart to stop beating.' My eyes are wet, my voice choked, and I'm vexed at her thoughts.

'Sail through with someone who gives it a meaning?' Presha says ruffling my hair with dead hand, her voice is muzzy, her eyes barely open; though, she tries to wrap up her pain with a broad smile on her face. She looks frail today.

'Nightingale, you are feeling drowsy. Why do you waste energy in empty talk? Better, sleep for some time. I know, anyways, it's difficult for you to talk sense without getting drunk.' I want to put a full stop on our conversation, there and then. Her thoughts are giving me the willies. I help her to lie straight and pull a blanket on her. As I turn around to flick off the light, she holds my hand with a force. I'm amazed to find the sudden stamina in her otherwise weak body. I stop and look at her.

She moves over a little, waves me with her hand to sit beside her.

'I was wrong when I said that if you want to know the real Presha, you'll find her in a pub. She was a restless Presha. Presha, who's talking to you now, is real Presha. Even, I wasn't aware of who I'm, till, the life I lived after losing you. And when I met Nikki, I realized what I should have been.

'Adie, you know, I always believed in the *cycle of birth*.'

'Oh! I never knew it!'

'No, I'm serious. You are born with a few scars, and some values ingrained in your soul, and with every birth soul also gets a chance to enrich itself.'

'Adie, I was born with some scars so entrenched in my soul that I couldn't think of anyone else above me. God has blessed me with loving and caring parents, but, but the scars on my soul have taken away the chance of enrichment in this birth. The Almighty gives you a chance to heal your scars by good deeds or karmas in this birth. Nikki made me discern that I failed on my karmas.'

'Relax Presha. I love you the way you are. Please don't stress yourself by talking so much.'

'Let me say what I want to– Nikki can be a perfect life partner for you. Marry her,' Presha says it as a commandment.

'Presha, I love you; I can't think of anyone else except you in this life,' I say, holding her hand; and catching her eyes.

'Adie, but I haven't loved you.' She withdraws her hand from mine, and closes her eyes; tears wetting her cheeks.

'No, you love me,' I'm baffled to hear what I was afraid of. She gives me jitters.

'If I loved you, I would have stayed with you; the way Nikki's doing. I abhorred you, for the way you treated me. I didn't trust you; that's why a few bad incidents could so easily shake my belief in your love.

'I never deserved you; if I couldn't stand by you in bad times, I don't have the right to enjoy your good times too,' Presha says, sobbing.

'You aren't wrong. There're moments in life when you make mistakes, so did you. It's human. I should have been more patient,' I say holding her hands, and coming closer to her.

'Adie, promise me– you'll not let your scars deny you the love that you deserve.'

'Presha, this is absurd! I don't believe in fancy philosophies.' I say, releasing her hand; and I want her to stop being namby-pamby.

'Do it for my sake.' Her eyes are pellucid as if she no longer sees this world.

'Okay, when you'll get well we'll talk about it,' I say, turning my back towards her so to hide my tears.

I wait for her to say something. There's no sound. I turn around to find her asleep. I switch off the light and slip in my bed beside her.

There's something which is making me restless. I get up in between and look at Presha. She's sleeping peacefully. Again, I close my eyes, but this is the worst night I ever had. A noise stirs me. I sweat profusely. I look around, but none is visible. I look at Presha, she's calm. I, lie down trying to contemplate what Presha was saying. I don't know when sleep sweeps me off.

Distant sounds by Ma wake me up. I look at Presha. She's still in slumber. She looks so innocent.

My heart beats with a thud. I don't know why, but I squeak, 'Presha, Presha...........,' there's no response. I'm turning blue. I shake her with gentle hands. She's still in sleep, sleep, from which she's never going to rise. I cry and cry. I yell, 'Maaa...' She scampers into the room. She looks at Presha, lying unconscious on the bed with hands fallen apart; she looks at me, drenched in a sea of tears. She's a mother; she knows Presha has gone forever. She sits beside Presha on the bed, holding her hands and caressing her hair. She's quiet, but her eyes are wet. She bends to kiss Presha on her forehead, as she would have done every morning to wake her up for school. She again bursts into tears to find her lifeless.

I'm standing with crossed arms, staring at my Nightingale, and tears rolling down my cheeks; feeling as helpless as Presha has always made me. Why did she come into my life if she had to go away from her life so soon?

* * * * *

Presha's gone from this world, but she is inside me. I'm feeling uneasy since I know she's not happy. She wants me to go out, find scars on my soul. Life would have been so easy if I could have gone with Presha. At times, I wonder– *if the God, as some people say, watching us from the celestial world, does best for everyone on this earth; or does he do something that gives him the best sadistic pleasures. If the latter was not true, he wouldn't have tied human beings together with an immortal bond of love; that, life becomes a curse if one soul unbinds itself from her body; and the others are ordered to breathe. He should have freed all the souls, concocted together, at the same time.*

I have to live, waiting for my pulse to stop. But till that happens, I can't sit with folded hands when I know my Presha is unquiet. I'll fulfill her every wish. If she likes so, I'll search for my scars.

I call up Dr. Sumer, 'Doc, you can plan for my past birth regression. But I need you to be there, I can't trust anyone else.'

'Good Adie. However, there's no guarantee that we'll find out anything from your past, or even if we'll be able to hypnotize you.'

'Sumer, I don't care. I know I need to go through this, my love wanted me to do it.'

'Adie, it totally depends on your willingness. The more you are ready to sink in altered state of consciousness, easier the job is.'

'I'm. I'm. I want her to feel happy.'

'Perfect, I'll try to fix the session after two weeks from now.'
'Bye Doc.'

I call up Nikki to tell her that I'm coming back to India. There's nothing left for me in Singapore. This time, I'll stay with my parents when I go back.

Nikki is there to receive me at the airport. Her eyes are wet, but there's a smile on her face. She looks sad. Never before I have seen her without eye makeup, she looks dull. She's grieved at my loss. Nikki hugs me lightly and looks at my face. Shrunken eyes and wrinkled skin reflect the infinite years I have lived in a month. I struggle to control my tears. Nikki can see through my eyes, but, but it's that time in life where she also knows, only time can be the healer.

I reach home, everyone there seems doleful; but why? They hardly met Presha, there can't be any feeling of personal loss. Are they grief-stricken 'cause I'm aggrieved, or, are they consoling me in anticipation of a bruised soul? Whatever! I don't want their sympathy. I'll do everything to make my Presha happy.

Nikki, I know, profoundly loves me; so it's hard for her to see me glum. Every day in the morning she comes to my home to meet me. Still, I haven't joined back the office; and I'll be working from home for some more time– till the time I feel I can face this world.

* * * * *

5 April 2011, Monday 11: 00 o'clock: We– Nikki, Presha and me, are at Sumer's clinic. Presha is wearing her blue jumpsuit, her eyes are dark and bold; hair flicks are falling on her face; with one hand, she tucks them behind her ears, and with the other she holds my hand tightly. She's so sure, my past birth wounds will be healed today, and maybe, then, I'll realize

how much she had always loved me. I tell her, no matter, she loved me or not, but I'll love her forever.

While I'm talking to Presha; Sumer introduces us to Dr. Tripathi, an expert in regression therapy. She looks serene, she has a velvety voice, good enough to create a magical spell on anyone's consciousness.

Suddenly, I find Presha has disappeared from the room. She wants me to believe in what I'm about to explore, sans any distraction.

'Adie, please relax yourself,' Dr. Tripathi says, with a smile.

I'm wearing cargo pants and a T-shirt. I lounge on the recliner; I know Presha's happy since I'm doing it.

'Close your eyes, Adie. Relax. Imagine the stress you feel melting away.

'Let the relaxation flow through your body, from head to arms to the tips of your fingers; and back to fingers-arms and head. Relax. Just relax!' Her voice is flowing through my body, it's soothing.

'Imagine you are sitting on a beach with a glass of red wine in your hand. You are alone and safe on this island. It's a bright sunny day. You are watching rolling in and out of the waves, bright blue waves.

'You take a sip of red wine. It flows throw your mouuth-stomachh-legggs-kneees-caaalves-toooes, tranquilizing everyyyy nerve. Relaxation flows back from toooes-caaalves-kneees-legggs-stomachh-mouuth.

'White crowns on the waves, advancing with the cool breeze are creating a magical impact on you.

'It's the end of a beautiful day and you are about to watch a sunset. Sun is drifting down, you are relaxing.

'Ten- down, Nine- deeper down, Eight- down as you relax, Seven, Six, Five, One- the sun has set completely and you are fully at ease. Wine glass in your hand is empty. You are relaxed.

'Now, you are going to embark on a journey, the journey of past life. As you are completely at ease; your mind is fresh, receptive to new ideas.

'Adie, I want you to imagine that you are standing on a lonely road. If you walk towards the right, you'll move into the future. If you walk towards left, you're moving into the past.

'I want you to start walking slowly facing the direction of the past.

'Have you started walking yet?'

'No.' I can hear and answer what the Doc asks.

'Please let me know when you start walking.

'I'm.'

'Okay. You are relaxed, at ease.

'You walk slowly, and then you increase your pace.

'You are about to enter a tunnel. When you come out on the other side of the tunnel, you'll enter into your past life, you choose to analyze.

'I want you to stop running when you are eighteen in your past life. Take a deep breath and look around.

'What do you see Adie?'

I'm quiet.

'Do you see anything?'

'River, field, trees…' I say in a intone voice.

'Which country is this?'

'India- Kerala.'

'Good.

'Is there someone with you?'

'No, but…

'I see my sister going down the path.'

'What else you see?'

'A few boys sitting on a tree.'

'Uh! What are they doing?'

'Throwing pebbles on my sister.'

'And what's she doing?

'Scarred, rushes towards the home.'

'What happens then?

'I beat them to death, a guy hit me on the forehead,' I say, pointing a finger to the left side of my forehead.

Dr. Tripathi looks at the pointed place, there's a small faint mark there– which is my birth mark. She smiles as it encourages her to go deeper down.

'Anything else; which you'll like to share.'

'I have a sister who's thirteen, God fearing mother and humble father.

'I go to college, my sister is in school…

'How's your relationship with your sister?'

'I love her. She's an innocent girl. She's my life.'

'Can you find some incident which drastically changed your life?'

I pause.

'My sister's turning eighteen today. The boy's family is visiting our home for her marriage proposal. I like the boy. He's good looking and well settled.'

'What happens then?'

'My sis isn't seen around in the house. Ma is upset.' My mouth is wide open; I'm fidgeting my fingers, swiveling my feet and my face is wet. I can't speak.

'Do you want us to stop here?'

'No.'

'Why are you so anxious?'

'I hear a knock at the front door. I open the door to find my sister and my foster uncle standing with their hands clasped; they are wearing garlands, they are married.'

'Who's this uncle?'

'Soul brother of our mother.'

'Where's Your Mom?

'She gets a paralytic attack and falls down on seeing them,' I say, with tears rolling down my cheeks; and my body is stiff.

'Have you talked to your sister? Why has she not confided in the family about it?'

'Dare she! She has committed a sin. He's our uncle.'

'But maybe she loves him, and she's scared to share it with you.'

I'm agitated. I bang the table with the fist.

'Are you okay?'

'No, I want to kill her.'

'What do you do then?'

'I slap her, and push her out of the house.'

'What happens to her?'

'I don't know. I have never met her after that.'

'How's life for you?'

'Miserable; my mother can't survive the shock for much long, she dies in a year.

'My father and I become the laughing stock of the people,' I say, biting my lips.

'Do you think your sister is wrong?'

'Yes, she hasn't followed the societal norms. He's our uncle.'

'She's an individual; what if she doesn't consider him so?

'Has she anytime reflected her feelings about him?'

'We never took it seriously, she was only a kid. She used to say he's my friend and not uncle; we all mocked at her when she said so.'

'So, she's honest; but she has done what she wanted to do.'

I'm swaying my head. My mouth is dry, I'm licking my lips. Doc asks me if we should stop the session. I can hear her, but my mind is not responding.

Doc asks, 'Is it wrong to live your life on your own terms?'

I'm weeping, I don't respond.

'It's perfectly okay. You are energetic to come back to your present life.

'You are Adie here. Adie, turn right; I want you to run fast to the tunnel.

'One- you are energetic, fast; two- faster, you are beaming with enthusiasm; three- you are flowing with energy. You are heeerre. Slllowly, open your eyes.

I open my eyes. My eyes are red. I see around; Presha's standing beside me, she's smiling.

I ask for my cell phone. Doc hands it to me. I call up Rachel.

She picks up the phone, and I just say *Sorry* in a choked voice. The phone drops down from my hand.

Doc asks me to relax on the chaise lounge.

I'm dumbfounded. Now, I can see Nikki is talking to me, but I can't hear her. She accompanies me to my house. I straightway enter my room and enclose myself there. I lie on the bed, observing everything; no thoughts crossing my head. My eyes fall on a picture– Rachel is wearing a pink party frock, and I'm in my black dress. She looks delighted, but I have a frown on my face.

I close my eyes and try to recollect about the picture. Tears flow down my eyes; I pull my hair and knock my head on the night table.

Rachel was ten years, and we two were invited to my best friend's birthday party. Rachel was so fond of my friend; she always treated him like a big brother. She got a new dress made for his birthday; and this picture was clicked by Muma when we were ready to leave for the party. I was upset to find Rachel, exuberant for the party as it was a boy's birthday. When we were going out, I don't know what happened to me, but there was a rush of blood and I slapped her. I yelled at Muma, for asking me to take her along with me to the party.

I accused Rachel of her intent of flirting with the boys there, and embarrassing me with her unscrupulous behavior. Rachel couldn't understand much of what I said, but she was crying, crying 'cause of the pain I had given to her. At that time I thought it was only the physical pain, but today, I can feel how much I tortured an innocent soul.

Yes, I deserve to live in this world; and each second of my life will be a punishment for me– it'll always remind me of the agony I have given to the people I loved the most. Rachel silently suffered throughout her life, but she never left me since I'm her brother; big brother; the ideal of her life.

I can feel my T-shirt is wet around my neck and sleeves. I wish I'm engulfed by this Tsunami.

Someone covers my eyes; I know this is Presha's fragrance. It's the party in Lime House, and Mike is taking out his wet shirt. I look at Presha; she steals her eyes from him as she's embarrassed. She faces him with shrinking eyes and raised Hands, showing her concern on the inconvenience caused to him. Mike blinks at her as if reassuring that she shouldn't spoil her day for such a small thing. This is what friends are for– to give you the support when you need it the most. I can hear myself sob.

Still, my eyes are closed, covered by her hands. She wants me to traverse to some other sins.

I ring the bell, Yuvi peeps into the eye view, and he talks to Presha; she opens the door, and Yuvi is standing behind her. Presha looks pale, she's trying to straighten her clenched face and her hand is swiveling on her stomach. It seems she has risen from a deep pain, and she's attempting to hold herself upright in front of me.

'Presha, please let me open my eyes. I can't see it anymore,' I screech at her.

'Adie, I'm sorry for the pain you are experiencing, but I need to get back my Adie,' Presha says moving her fingers in my hair.

'Presha come back. I know you can. I want to cherish this life with you. I promise, with my heeled soul, you'll find me the best husband on this earth.

'Nightingale, please release me from the vicious cycle of a wounded soul. If I'm not telling you in this life that how much I love you, and how fortunate I'm to have you as my love, I'll be again born with scars on my soul.

'Please forgive me, and come back. I can't live without you.'

'Adie, like everyone else, I also had a destiny. I have paid for my karmas.

'You, still have to live your destiny. Your love is Nikki; lead a happy life with her.'

'I don't love her, I love you.'

'Adie, I have seen an immense love for her in your eyes. You just need to realize it. Above all, none can love you the way she loves you. She loved you and stood by you in your distressed time. Now she deserves to be with you in the best of your times,' Presha waves at me, she glitters like a star.

I hear Muma slam the door, and call out my name. I turn my face towards Presha. She isn't there. I'm sure, she was here. We spoke heart to heart last night, and I confessed to her that she's the white rose in my garden. She was ecstatic at the thought.

'Oh, God! Why have you done it to me?' I whine. Muma is calling my name loudly, she's afraid if anything is wrong.

How can things go wrong? I'm love of a girl who always lived her life on her own terms; and even when she has left this world, she's doing what she wants to do. So, how can I run away from life and not do what I want to do? I open the door. Muma looks at me; tears wetting her cheeks and mine too.

She embraces me; two of us stand there, mesmerized by the intricacies of human life. Her son is reborn after thirty-three years, and I know what I want in life after losing everything.

I open my eyes, unfold Muma's arms; I cup her face in my hand, and wipe off her tears. I turn my face towards the lady, standing some distance away from us.

I move towards her, hold her hand and kneel in front of her,

'Nikki, can I be a pleasant surprise of your life which is waiting to unfold? Teach me, what love is?'

She bends down, looks into my eyes and hugs me for a lifetime…

* * * * *

To love someone is– to be with him in his rough times; be the panacea for his life, and lead him to those magnificent moments, which you always dreamt to cherish with him. Love has a mystical power to heal every scar on the soul.

Printed in the United States
By Bookmasters